DEMONS IN THE DUNES

PIERCE MOSTYN PARANORMAL INVESTIGATIONS
BOOK 6

C W HAWES

CWH BOOKS

For Jodi and Susannah,
and Jack Koblas, who's gone but not forgotten

ENTER THE IMAGINATIVE WORLD OF CW HAWES

Enter my world. A world of terror on a cosmic scale. Just click, tap, or scan the QR code below.

Fear is the most primal of human emotions. And fear of the unknown is the most terrifying of all fears.

If you are new to the Pierce Mostyn Paranormal Investigations series, then *Demon in the Dunes* is an excellent entry point into the series and into my world.

In addition to my Pierce Mostyn Paranormal Investigations books, I've written short stories set in the world of the macabre and arcane. Many of which are only available to folks on my mailing list.

So just click, tap, or scan the QR code to enter my world of terror and the macabre. You will get a free copy of *The Feeder* and you'll get my monthly email of news and curated contact. Terror awaits!

1

IRAM OF THE OLD ONES

SPECIAL AGENT in Charge Pierce Mostyn gathered up his parachute and watched the giant Lockheed cargo plane fly off in a northerly direction back to Doha, Qatar, and the US air base there.

Mostyn surveyed the desert. Resting on the sand were three Humvees and their trailers, along with four crates of equipment, which contained food, water, fuel, weapons, tools, tents, and ammunition. He watched the eleven members of his team gather in their parachutes. If there was room, they'd take the chutes with them. If not, they'd be buried to avoid discovery.

The sun was bright and even with his tinted goggles on, Mostyn had to shade his eyes with his hand. He took in the geography where they'd been dropped by the plane. The single thing that impressed itself on his mind was the sheer aloneness of the place. The Empty Quarter was very much true to its name. A desolate wasteland of sand and more sand, and very little besides sand.

The sun was burning hot. *Of all the times to come to this godforsaken place it had to be August*, Mostyn thought.

The time wasn't even noon and the temperature was already a hundred and one in the shade — only there wasn't any shade.

Special Agent DC Jones, who could easily pass for a Greek god, was directing the unpacking of the crates and the loading of the trailers. Mostyn decided to join the other team members.

Unlike Jones, Mostyn, even with his short strawberry blond hair, could walk through a crowd and no one would remember seeing him. For this mission, he had traded in his custom-made suit for a pair of khakis and a khaki colored linen shirt. A pith helmet protected his head from the sun.

"Hey, Boss, decided to get your hands dirty?" Jones said, a twinkle in his eye.

"Nope," Mostyn replied. "I'm wearing gloves."

Willie Lee Baker, the team photographer, laughed. "Gotcha there, Jones."

"That's not difficult to do," Doctor Dotty Kemper, one of the world's foremost forensic anthropologists, said. Like Mostyn, she'd traded in her suit for a pair of khakis. Unlike Mostyn, she wore knee-high black boots, and a large straw hat to cover her head. Some of her dark hair, cut in a Dutch Bob, was visible under the hat.

"I see," Jones replied, "it's gang up on DC time. That's okay. Go ahead. Just remember who will save your asses when the shit hits the fan."

Special Agent Kymbra NicAskill gave Jones a playful shove. "Gee, thanks, Jonesy, for the shoutout."

"What are you talking about, Nicky?" Jones said. "I'm the one who saves their bacon. You're the new kid, remember?"

From one crate over, Special Forces Agent Donovan White said, "Are you people over there going to get any work done?"

Jones shot back, "Do you even know the meaning of the word, Don?"

Appearing out of thin air, Helene Dubreuil, who looked human, but wasn't *homo sapiens*, or at least any variety of *homo sapiens* evolved on earth, was holding a lizard. "Look, Mostyn Pierce, isn't this the most interesting creature?"

"Are you sure that thing isn't poisonous?" Doctor Richard Munroe, the linguist said.

"I do not know," Helene replied. "It is so pretty." She set the lizard on the ground and it scampered away.

And on the banter went. All the while the team unloaded the crates and transferred the equipment to the trailers. When the trailers were loaded, they were hitched to the Humvees.

"Okay, listen up, everyone," Mostyn called out. "Jones, you'll drive the lead vehicle. Neumeyer, Doctor Hyde, and Baker, you're with Jones. I will drive the middle vehicle. Dotty, Helene, and Salih, you three are with me. NicAskill, you're last in line. White, Doctor Lentz, and Doctor Munroe, you're with NicAskill. The site is about twenty klicks north of our current position. When we get to the site, we'll set up camp outside the city. Any questions?"

Mostyn's eyes swept the group, and, seeing none, he said, "Let's move out."

———

The Rub' al Khali, the famous Empty Quarter of the Arabian Peninsula, is a vast expanse of sand dunes and salt flats; some quarter of a million square miles. Several Arab tribes call the region home. None of them in the area where Mostyn found himself.

Sitting next to him was Salih ibn Adi, a twenty-seven-year-old second generation Arab-American who was studying for his doctorate in anthropology. His special interest was the culture of the Empty Quarter tribes. He was the team's translator.

Sitting behind Mostyn was Doctor Dotty Kemper and sitting next to her was Helene Dubreuil. Helene was tall and very feminine, with alabaster skin and waist-length black hair that she wore in a ponytail. However, if anyone mistook that femininity for weakness, they were in for a big surprise.

Helene was born some nine or ten centuries ago in the deep subterranean world of K'n-yan, whose inhabitants came to earth eons ago with the Great Old Ones. The K'n-yanians were in many ways superior to *homo sapiens*. However, over the ages, they had become indolent, depraved, and sadistic. And when Mostyn and his team were captured by the K'n-yanians on a previous mission, Helene was the one who'd saved them from almost certain death. A hideously horrible death, at the hands of her people. When Mostyn's team was rescued, she came to the surface world with them.

Both Helene and Dotty were in a relationship with Mostyn, and if Dotty could help it, not with each other. All three suspected the director of the Office of Unidentified Phenomena, Doctor Rafe Bardon, to be the culprit behind the three agreeing to such an arrangement. "Him and his goddamned ancient Egyptian magic," as Dotty often said. Helene, however, didn't mind the threesome one bit.

Mostyn looked at the endless piles of sand. The Humvees were having some difficulty negotiating them, and he was thinking they might have an easier journey if they took a different route. He picked up the radio's handset.

"H one, this is H two. Over."

"Read you loud and clear, Boss. Over." Jones's voice.

"The driving is a bit difficult. Do you think you can find some hard-packed earth, instead of all this sand? Over."

"Already checked. It would add days to our trip and we don't have the supplies for the extra time. Over."

"Okay. Thanks, Jones. Mostyn out."

Salih chuckled. "Camels. Should've used camels. If Allah had meant for cars and trucks to be used in the desert, he would have given them to the Arabs in the first place."

From the back seat, came Dotty's voice, "That's a crock of shit."

Salih, his bearded face displaying a huge grin, replied, "They don't call us camel jockeys for nothing."

Helene, a bit of puzzlement in her voice, said, "Does that mean I shouldn't drive because my people didn't invent a car?"

"No, it doesn't mean that," Dotty told her. "It means Arabs will use any excuse to reinforce their Medieval thinking."

"PC, Dot," Mostyn said.

"Don't worry about it, Mr. Mostyn," Salih said, "I'm not offended." He turned to Dotty. "Women can now drive in the Kingdom. They're just as modern as you."

"That's a load of road apples," Dotty shot back. "Your king just did that so you could attract tourists. Money for when you run out of oil."

Salih laughed. "He's not my king, and it's not my oil. I'm an American."

"What are road apples?" Helene asked.

Laughter erupted in the Humvee.

Dotty touched her arm. "I'll tell you later."

Mostyn cursed as the Humvee slid sideways down the dune. He gave the vehicle more gas and powered it back up so he was once again in formation.

"Doctor Bardon should've listened to me," Salih said.

"If he had, I wouldn't be here," Dotty countered. After a pause, she said, "Come to think of it, I wish he had."

"What do you mean, Dot? You've been complaining about not having a mission in the city. Now you have one."

"Fork you, Mostyn."

Helene was all smiles. "If you weren't here, you wouldn't have all of these new experiences."

"That's fine," Dotty replied. "Traipsing around this great big sandbox is an experience I can do without."

Mostyn looked out at the vast expanse of the dunes. There was a certain beauty to this sea of sand. Yet, at the same time, there was the terror of it too. He thought of the lines by Coleridge: "water, water everywhere,/nor any drop to drink." Only in this case, it was sand everywhere and no water to drink. Being alone in the Rub' al Khali was much like being alone in the ocean treading water. Death was only a matter of time.

Salih intruded on his thoughts. "Do you think, Mr. Mostyn, this mission will be as easy as Doctor Bardon made it sound?"

"Bardon makes everything sound easy, so, no, I don't think it will be easy. If the ancient legends are true, then Iram of the pillars was one of the gateways by which the Great Old Ones invaded our universe. And if the gateway, all these eons later, is still open…" Mostyn shrugged.

"It is said King Shaddad and his people were giants and that they built Iram to challenge Allah. That Iram was to be a paradise on Earth perhaps even greater than Allah's paradise in heaven. And when the city was completed, just as King Shaddad was about to enter it, Allah sent a huge sandstorm that wiped away the king, his people, and the city."

"That's some legend," Mostyn said. "When did this happen?"

"Supposedly before Adam. It is also claimed by several obscure and arcane traditions and in some Sufi traditions, that Iram existed on several planes and was a doorway to the Void. In support of those traditions is the fact that Iram of the pillars, can be translated as Iram of the Old Ones."

Mostyn nodded. "And the Great Old Ones came across the Void to claim this dimension for their own, and will do so again when they are awakened and the time is right."

"If the old ones of the traditions are the same as these Great Old Ones you are speaking of, does Doctor Bardon know what he is doing?"

"Usually," Mostyn replied, a smile tugging at the corner of his lips.

"My people came with the Great Old Ones many ages ago," Helene said, "but we do not know of this Iram."

"Maybe you call it something else," Dotty said.

"We simply crossed the Void and entered this world through the gate."

"I think at that point, the gate and the legends match, regardless of what the gate is called," Mostyn said.

"Yes, you are without a doubt correct, my husband," Helene replied.

"Will you stop calling him that?" Dotty said, irritation coloring her tone.

"But he is, my sister, just as much as he is *your* husband."

"Oh my God!" Salih exclaimed. "You have two wives, Mr. Mostyn?"

A red flush began creeping into Mostyn's face. "You might say that. Back to your original question, Salih, no, I don't think this mission will be easy. I've never been on an easy mission."

Dotty chimed in. "There are no easy missions in the Office of Unidentified Phenomena. None whatsoever." After a pause, she added, "Unless you're dead."

Mostyn braked. Up ahead, Jones's Humvee had stopped, and Mostyn pulled up next to it. NicAskill brought her vehicle to a stop next to Mostyn's.

From the top of the sand mountain, they looked out over a valley which had been exposed by what could only be called the sandstorm of the century. This was what the OUP satellites had photographed, and Doctor Bardon had been so very excited about.

Before them, filling the valley, was an immense city. Everyone got out of the Humvees and stood staring at the ancient ruins spreading out before them. No one spoke. The scene defied speech.

Mostyn's eyes took in the city. It was spectacular, even with all the hallmarks of the ravages of time, and he couldn't help but notice that it wasn't quite right. It's lines and angles and the geometric shapes didn't quite fit those of any city on Earth. There was a decidedly alien quality to this site. Human engineering alone had not imagined the design of the structures or the layout of the city itself, and Mostyn guessed that not all of the hands that built it had been human.

After several moments, Helene fell to her knees and said, "This is the gateway. This is the door through which my people came to this world." And then she prostrated herself before the ancient ruin.

2

THE HOUSE OF SATAN

THE VALLEY RAN east to west and was surrounded by mountains of sand, except on the east. There the valley emptied into a salt flat that still had remnants of water in it from the rains produced by Cyclone Mekunu.

Mostyn directed the team to make camp on the east end of the valley, near the salt flat. After three hours a tent village could be seen that was dwarfed not only by the mountains of sand, but by the immense ruin of Iram itself.

With the camp set up, Mostyn called for a working lunch. The midday meal provided courtesy of the US military and their MRE packets.

"Okay people, we're here. We have five days to gather as much information as we can. We'll form two teams. Our archaeologists, Doctors Maddy Hyde and Waldemar Lentz, will be the team leaders.

"Special Agent NicAskill and Special Forces Agent Neumeyer, you are with Doctor Hyde. Special Agent Jones and Special Forces Agent White, you are with Doctor Lentz.

"The rest of you will rotate. You'll spend two and a half

days with one team and two and a half days with the other. Doctor Munroe and Ms. Dubreuil will start with Doctor Hyde. Mr. Baker and Doctor Kemper will start with Doctor Lentz.

"Salih and I will be roving. We'll deal with any unexpected visitors. Any questions?"

Doctor Richard Munroe spoke. "This operation would've run a whole lot smoother if we had more people."

"Not my call, Doc," Mostyn said. "However, given the current tense relations between Washington and Riyadh, this is probably the best we could get. Remember, the Saudis don't know the real reason we're here. We're scientists from MIT checking on the aftermath of the cyclone. Any other questions?"

"Do we have any real food?" Doctor Dotty Kemper asked.

"MREs are real food, Dot," Mostyn replied.

"By who's definition?"

"The US government."

Dotty blew a raspberry and folded her arms across her chest.

"Any other questions?" Mostyn asked, while looking over the group. "Okay, seeing none, I'd like for you all to take a preliminary look at your areas of operation. Doctor Lentz, your team will work on the west end of the city. Doctor Hyde, you and your people are on the east. Finish eating and move out."

The team members finished eating, deposited the mylar packets and biodegradable eating utensils in the trash containers, and departed. While Mostyn watched them leave, Salih walked up to him.

"What do we do, Mr. Mostyn?"

"We're going to circulate and run interference should any

unwanted visitors show up. Is that okay with you? Or would you rather be with a team?"

"No. What would I do? I'm a translator. There won't be anything for me to translate in these ruins."

"Okay. Good." However, Mostyn could tell something was bothering the young man. "Something else on your mind?"

"If I'm honest with you, Mr. Mostyn, I'd rather not be here at all. This place just feels, well, evil."

"You won't get any argument from me there. Evil is what the OUP deals with. Come on."

Mostyn and Salih walked out of the tent that served as both the mess tent and the community tent to where the Humvees and trailers were parked. Sitting there was a small ATV. Mostyn got on.

"Sit behind me, Salih. We're going for a ride."

The Arab-American smiled and climbed on. Mostyn started up the machine and off they went. From the camp to the edge of the city, which oddly enough had no walls, was five hundred yards. Mostyn pushed the little machine as fast as it would go across the hard-packed sand of the valley floor. The little engine making a whine that reverberated and echoed off the ancient walls and columns of the buildings, breaking a silence that had reigned over the city and the site of its burial for millennia.

Mostyn drove the ATV down what appeared to be the main thoroughfare from what he guessed would have been the waterfront into the central city square. He stopped and turned off the engine.

"Come on, Salih, let's look around."

Salih got off the ATV and took a look at the buildings surrounding the city square. "Something's not right here, Mr. Mostyn. These buildings, they... they don't look normal."

Mostyn looked at the buildings and then turned his gaze to what must've been, at one time, an enormous fountain. He slowly walked around the structure. "You're right, Salih, this place isn't normal. Something alien had a hand in its design and probably even in its construction." He stopped and gazed at the tall fountain. "If this thing was actually a fountain, it'd mean that there must've been water here at one time. Lots of water."

Salih nodded. "Yes. The entire Empty Quarter was in very ancient times extremely green. The frankincense trade originated down in Oman and ran through here. Then the climate changed and it became a wasteland."

"Climate change before greenhouse gases. Interesting. Do we know what caused the climate to change?"

Salih shook his head. "I don't think so. Just like we don't really know why the Sahara became a desert." After a pause, he continued, "But this place..." He spread his arms and turned in a circle to indicate the city. "This place was cursed by Allah. The sand here is a curse."

"A curse? Do you actually believe that? I thought, having been born and raised in America, gone to college, you'd be—"

"Less of a fanatic?"

"I was going to say much more secular."

"I may be much more secular than my parents, but I do practice my religion, Mr. Mostyn, and hope that I am a pious man. It is how my parents raised me: to believe in Allah and His prophet. And I do. It is the least I can do to honor them."

"I see."

"I spent two years with the Bedouins in Oman. Their lives are pretty simple. They have their religion, their traditions, and the daily business of trying to survive. They also have legends, ancient legends, about this place. And superstitions.

They say it is cursed and that Allah, in His mercy, cursed it with the sand."

"And you believe that?"

"I do. I think it fits with the Qur'an."

"I see. So why did you come on this mission?"

"Doctor Bardon told me this was, to use his words, 'Purely a reconnaissance mission, young man, purely reconnaissance.' And I believed him. He said my knowledge of the Bedouins and their language would be a great help. Why wouldn't I believe him?"

A smile tugged at the corners of Mostyn's mouth. "Yes, why wouldn't you?"

"But I don't think Doctor Bardon told me the truth."

"Let's put it this way: he told you his version of the truth."

"His version? There is only one truth."

"Not in Bardon's world. May I ask why you joined the OUP?"

Salih laughed, although there was a trace of bitterness in the laughter. "Doctor Bardon made me an offer I couldn't refuse. He said my education would be paid for, and I'd have this incredible salary and amazing benefits. A lifetime of guaranteed employment." Salih shrugged. "My parents aren't rich. They've struggled their entire lives. I'm their only son and it's my duty to provide for them in their old age."

Mostyn couldn't help but notice the gold rings on Salih's hands. Three fairly large ones at that. He thought, *He may be providing for his parents, but he isn't denying himself either.*

To Salih, he said, "Bardon can be very persuasive. But why did he pick you to begin with? There's something in your life that he found out about that makes you a perfect candidate for the Office of Unidentified Phenomena and the work we do. What is it?"

"My family are Sufis, Muslim mystics. I have studied the works of Ibn Arabi and al-Ghazali, the greatest of Muslim mystics, since I was eighteen. When I was twenty-five, my soul crossed the Void to the realms of light. I have been a regular traveler ever since, gradually going higher and higher in the planes of existence."

"And Bardon found out and recruited you."

"Yes."

Mostyn chuckled to himself and thought, *A pious man who likes big gold rings. Where have I encountered that before?*

His eyes looked up and down the tall column that formed the center of the fountain. Any images that had been there were long ago worn away by the sand. All that remained was the conically shaped black pillar. The circular terraces that must have held pools of water at one time were likewise just bare black stone.

"When this thing was working, it must've been amazing," Mostyn said. "Come on, we have work to do. Let's go and take a look at some of these buildings."

With Salih following, Mostyn headed for a large black building, which had many massive pillars across the front. Two-dozen steps led up to the portico, an expansive area between the pillars and the front of the building.

Everything seemed off about the structure. The steps were not made for the average size human. The rise was too high and the steps themselves too broad. The columns and lines of the building didn't follow Euclidean geometry. They were off. How so, Mostyn couldn't put his finger on it. The effect, though, was immediate. A certain uneasiness wrapped itself around him. He could tell Salih felt it too.

"This place was made for giants," Salih said, a touch of awe in his voice.

"Which would confirm your legends."

"Yes, it does. The legends are real."

"I'd say, it confirms the legends are based on reality. No legend is real. That's why it's a legend and not history."

If Salih heard him, he gave no indication. He simply stood there mesmerized by the gargantuan structure.

"Come on, let's see what's inside." Mostyn started up the steps, and with a bit of non-verbal coaxing got Salih to follow him.

With some difficulty, the two climbed the stairs and reached the portico.

While Mostyn looked up and down the length of the shaded expanse, Salih, awe in his voice, said, "This place truly was made by giants, Mr. Mostyn. Look at the size of these doors!"

Mostyn took in the massive doors before them. The pair still showed evidence of the ornate carving that had once decorated them. Mostyn whistled.

"They are big, I'll grant you that. Although giant doors were often used to impress visitors, not that they were actually needed for the inhabitants."

"But these are thirty feet tall. And look at how wide they are. They wouldn't need to be that big to impress people."

Mostyn shrugged. "You might have a point there." With Salih in tow, he walked up to the doors. Attached to the left door was a wide strip of gold that overlapped the other door where they met.

"Let's see if these will open," Mostyn said.

The two men pushed on the righthand one, and, after much effort, got the massive wooden door to swing inward on protesting hinges just enough for them to enter. With Mostyn in the lead, the two men walked into the building.

Light filtered into the enormous interior from large open windows that were located high up near the roof. Sand had filled in about a third of the floor on each side of the building. The wide center aisle remained mostly clear.

Lining both sides of the center aisle were rows of massive statues, and even in the dim light Mostyn could tell that they represented hideous things. Things not of this dimension.

The sand on each side of the building formed a gentle curve from the bottom of the windows to the bases of the statues, giving something of a bowl effect to the building's interior.

"It's too dark to see much of anything," Salih said. "We should've brought flashlights."

"Maybe it's a good thing we didn't."

"Don't you want to see what this place is?"

"I think I already know."

"You do?"

"Yes. It's what might be called The Hall of the Great Old Ones."

"What do you mean?"

"These statues here?"

"Yes?"

"If I'm not mistaken, they're statues of the Great Old Ones."

"You mean..."

"Yes, I do."

Even in the dim light, Mostyn could tell Salih's eyes were like saucers. Barely above a whisper, Mostyn heard him say "Ya Allah!"

And after a brief span of silence, Salih cried out, "We've walked into the house of the Shaytan! Rahimana Allah!" He turned and ran from the building.

3

THE HALL OF THE GREAT OLD ONES

MOSTYN WATCHED the young man run from the building, but when he heard the faint sound of the ATV's engine, he cursed and ran out to the portico just in time to see the dust hanging in the air from the fleeing translator.

He shook his head and promised himself to have a come to Jesus meeting with Salih when he got back to camp.

So much for going to an American university, he thought. Out loud he said, "He's going to have to keep his religious superstition in check if he's going to work for the OUP".

Mostyn watched the wind dispel the dust cloud from the long-vanished ATV. He just might have to have a discussion with Doctor Bardon about installing a more rigorous vetting process. It's one thing to take on someone who's had visions of the Void. *Positive* visions. It's quite another to put that person face to face with the dark realities of the Void.

Taking a deep breath of the hot desert air, and blowing it back out, he turned and re-entered the building.

"At least it's somewhat cooler in here," he said to the silent stone images. Hideous images. And he was glad they were silent.

In spite of what he'd said to Salih, Mostyn was never without the small flashlight he carried for emergencies. He took it out and turned it on. The little beam of light seemed to lose itself in the darkness of the shadows. No, that wasn't quite right. It was more as though the darkness absorbed the light and made it its own.

Mostyn flashed the little light around. "This is next to worthless," he muttered and turned it off. But rather than go back to camp and get a more powerful lamp, he decided to explore the great hall as best he could. After all he was there and had nowhere else to be. At least for the time being.

The dim light filtering in from the high windows didn't help much to define what it was Mostyn was looking at. If anything, it was as though it created rather than eliminated the shadows. Almost as if its purpose was to obscure the hellish hall's interior.

Mostyn walked down the center of the building until he reached the far end. There he encountered a raised stage. In the center of the stage appeared to be another tall structure, perhaps a dais of some sort. The shadows were too deep and his flashlight too weak for him to determine with any precision what it was he was looking at. In addition, the persistent off-ness, the sense that the lines and angles and surfaces were not quite right by human standards, tended to blur what he was seeing. As though he had an uncorrected astigmatism.

He walked to the eastern end of the stage. It was partially buried in sand. He turned around and saw light beginning to stream in from the western windows. He walked to the west side of the hall and stopped when he reached the sand, and turned around. The light was beginning to illuminate the gigantic and horrific images, and it was as he suspected. This was indeed the Hall of the Great Old Ones.

He looked at the hideously blasphemous statues. The air suddenly seemed cold, very cold, and full of a malevolence that was old when this universe was young. Mostyn shivered. A chill crept over him; a chill that made the lifeless vacuum of black outer space feel warm by comparison.

———

When Mostyn got back to camp, he sought out Salih and found him in their tent praying. He thought for a moment about how he should proceed with the young man, and decided he needed to tackle the issue head on. Gently, yet firmly. He entered the tent and sat on a stool, waiting for the young Sufi mystic to finish his prayers.

When he came up from his final prostration, he saw Mostyn and embarrassment colored his face.

"I'm sorry, Mr. Mostyn. I panicked."

"I know you did. I was there, remember?"

Salih hung his head, and Mostyn continued, "You also left me in the lurch. We're a team, Salih. Team members cover for each other. No matter what. Even if you're so scared, you're pissing and crapping your pants, you stick with your teammates."

"Yes, sir. I'm sorry, sir. It won't happen again."

"Are you sure?"

"Yes, sir. I've prayed and asked Allah to protect me and the team from the Shaytan, and to give me courage so that I'm not a disappointment to my parents, or to you, or to Doctor Bardon."

Mostyn nodded. He studied the young man; and, while he

himself wasn't religious, he'd just seen too many things, too much of what was behind the veil of reality to believe in pious myths, if Salih's belief system helped him, he wasn't going to question it. Then again, in actuality, how pious was the young man if he sported those gold rings? Rather ostentatious for someone trying to get close to God. Perhaps his religion was more ritual than heartfelt. After all, that's how it was with most religious people. Cultural faith. In Salih's defense, he was young, and now flush with money. Why not splurge a little? No one was consistent.

Finally Mostyn said, "I won't put this in my report."

"Thank you, sir."

"This is your first field assignment?"

"Yes, sir, it is."

"The Office of Unidentified Phenomena deals with all manner of odd, unusual, and unexplained things. Some of what we encounter is downright terrifying. It's okay to be afraid. Just don't let fear get in the way of your duty."

"Yes, sir."

"One other thing. Aside from fear, there is temptation."

"What do you mean, sir?"

"Just what I said. We encounter all manner of things. Talismans. Magic formulas. Gold and gems. Things that tempt one with wealth and power. They are worse than fear. They corrupt the soul. They will niggle out every hidden weakness in your being. Treat them as poison. Because they will kill you. Fear won't kill you unless you do something stupid. But temptation will send you to the pit faster than you can say *astagh-firu lillah*. Do you understand?"

"Yes, sir."

"Good. See to it that you don't forget."

"I won't, sir." The young Arab-American paused, then asked, "You know Arabic?"

"I know a little bit of everything."

Salih nodded, although there was a trace of puzzlement on his face.

Mostyn smiled and left the tent in search of the radio. He wanted to send a preliminary report to Bardon on his findings.

The radio tent was off to the side of the camp, marked by a tall antenna that rose out of the ground next to it. He entered, turned on the set, and tapped out his message on the computer, which automatically encrypted it before sending. When finished, he exited the tent and walked a short distance out onto the salt flat. The only sound was the faint hum of the generator.

Even as the sun headed for the western horizon and the giant piles of sand began casting long shadows, the air was still hot, and heat waves shimmered off the barren tract of land before him.

Compare this place to a rain forest, he thought. *Both are beautiful. Both are deadly. Both inhospitable. Yet somehow humans eke out an existence.*

"What a resilient species we are," he murmured. "But are we more resilient than those blasphemies of un-nature who want to muscle us out of our turf?"

He stared out at the billion scintillant diamonds reflecting the sun. After a time, he shrugged. "I guess only time will tell."

He turned around, and walked back to the camp.

————

After dinner Mostyn held a team meeting. He began by calling on Doctor Lentz to report what he found.

"The west end of the city is not fully clear of sand," Lentz began. "In fact, many of the buildings are still almost completely buried. To uncover them will take months."

"What percent are explorable right now?" Mostyn asked.

"I'd say thirty percent are completely open. Around forty percent are partially buried. Some more. Some less. The remaining thirty percent are either nearly buried or completely buried."

"If they're completely buried, how do you know they're there?" Doctor Munroe asked.

"From estimating where the city border would be," Lentz replied.

"Because we have limited time available to us," Mostyn said, "I want your group, Doctor Lentz, to focus on the city center."

"Those buildings by the fountain?" Lentz asked.

"Yes," Mostyn replied.

"Very well. First thing in the morning."

Mostyn turned to Doctor Hyde. "What did you find?"

"Most of the buildings appeared to be residences, or places of business. I think the salt flat was once a lake. We found a couple boats and evidence of fishing activity."

"Is it worth our time for your team to continue there?" Mostyn asked.

"We can learn about the people who lived here," Hyde replied. "For example, in several of the houses we found altars and idols. The idols will give us an idea if the families had their own household gods and goddesses, or if the city had one set of deities that everyone worshipped."

Mostyn reflected on her comment for a moment before

speaking. "For now, keep working on the east side of the city. That might prove to be useful information. We'll re-evaluate tomorrow after you've had a full day to explore." His eyes took in the entire team before he continued.

"Salih and I looked at one of the buildings in the central square. I think it's safe to say we could call the place the Hall of the Great Old Ones. The building may have been the main temple of Iram. It may also mask the actual location of the gate between our world and their world. Doctor Lentz I want your team to focus on that building. Your job is to prove or disprove my guess."

"Sounds good to me," he replied.

"Ms. Dubreuil, I want you to work with Doctor Lentz tomorrow."

"Yes, Mostyn Pierce."

"We have limited time. Nature, at least Doctor Bardon thinks it was nature, has uncovered the city. We need to ascertain if the gate is still open, or if it is closed."

"And if it is open?" Jones asked.

"Then we must close it, or destroy it," Mostyn replied.

Jones rubbed his hands together, a gleam in his eyes.

"Don't get too happy, Jones," Mostyn said. "We aren't blowing up anything yet."

"Nothing wrong in hoping, Boss," Jones said, a big grin on his face.

Dotty Kemper raised her hand.

"Go ahead, Doctor Kemper," Mostyn said.

"What I found odd was that we didn't come across any bodies, or skeletons. Did you, Doctor Hyde?"

"Now that you mention it, no, we didn't."

Dotty continued, "It's as though everyone just disappeared."

Salih, his voice trembling, said, "King Shaddad and his people were evil. This place is evil. Allah took them and buried this place to save the world from the evil. And now we are here."

"This place is the gate," Helene countered. "It is a door between this world and the world my people came from. This place is not evil. Just as a door is not evil. But what may be on either side of the door, that is what you will find to be evil."

Mostyn opened his mouth to speak, but, before he could get a word out, a wind sprang up that caused the sides and the roof of the tent to flap with a loud snapping sound. Then the lights went out.

4

NATURAL OR SUPERNATURAL

THE DARKNESS WAS FILLED with curses, shouting, a scream, and plenty of shuffling. In a moment, Mostyn's flashlight provided a bit of light. Then flashlights from Jones, NicAskill, Neumeyer, and White lit up the inside of the tent. The wind continued to make the tent fabric flap and snap.

"Neumeyer, White, check the generator to make sure it's running," Mostyn ordered. "Jones, NicAskill, check to see if we've had visitors."

The special agents and special forces personnel left. To the rest of the team, Mostyn said, "The only one here who hasn't been in the field before now is Salih. You all know stuff happens on these missions. I expect you to act like the experienced professionals you are."

He turned to Salih. "And you…"

Salih hung his head in shame.

"You need to get your act together. I want no more talk about evil. Do you hear me?"

Salih nodded.

"I can't hear you."

Salih looked up at Mostyn. "Yes, sir."

"Good. The Great Old Ones might appear to be evil. We might think of them as malevolent entities. But that is from our perspective. From theirs, we're simply a nuisance. Like having ants in the house. That being said, do *we* want *them* here? No, we don't. This is *our* home. And we protect what is ours. So let's keep our wits about us, and do our mission. Even though they don't know it, our country and the world are depending on us. Have I made myself clear?"

There was a chorus of yeses in response.

"Good."

Jones and NicAskill returned.

"Anything?" Mostyn asked.

"Not that we found, sir," NicAskill replied.

Mostyn nodded. "Probably not intruders."

Another minute went by and the lights came back on.

"Let there be light," Jones quipped.

"Didn't take you for a Bible reader," Baker said.

"Is that from the Bible?" Jones asked.

Baker shook his head. "I don't know about you, Jones."

"What do you mean, Willie Lee?" Jones said, and added, "I bet *you* don't know everything."

Neumeyer and White entered the tent. "The generator ran out of gas," Neumeyer said. "Nothing to worry about on that score."

"But with the wind kicking up the sand," White said, "we might want to shut it down. Sand can ruin a piece of machinery faster than a blowtorch going through cardboard."

Mostyn nodded. "You and Neumeyer shut it down and cover it up."

The two men departed and Mostyn addressed the rest of the team. "Let's call it a night. Everyone to your tents. Use flashlights and the battery lamps as little as possible. We don't want to run out of batteries, and until the wind dies down, we won't be able to recharge them. Meeting's over. Goodnight."

Everyone filed out and went to one of the three tents. Helene and Dotty waited to go out with Mostyn, and, when everyone was gone, each of the women took one of Mostyn's hands in theirs.

"At least Herndon won't have his shorts in a knot over hotel accommodations on this trip," Dotty said.

Mostyn laughed. "The little bean counter was dithering over tent size when I saw him."

"Oh, for crying out loud!" Dotty said. "Goddamn accountants."

"There is not a lot of room in the tents," Helene said. "How does one live in them?"

"Haven't you ever been in a tent?" Dotty asked.

"No, my sister. I did not know what a tent was until we set them up here. They are very flimsy dwellings."

Dotty laughed. "Put that in your report, Mostyn. The special consultant says the tents are very flimsy."

"For all the good it will do," Mostyn replied.

Dotty kissed Mostyn. "Goodnight, Pierce. Keep a watch on that Arab. He's stretched pretty tight."

"He's an American, Dot."

"Yeah, right."

"Dot." Mostyn's voice implied the reprimand.

"Yeah, yeah, I know. All that PC shit. Goodnight, Mostyn." And she gave him another kiss.

"Goodnight, my husband." Helene kissed Mostyn on the cheek. She turned to Dotty, slipped her arm around her waist, and said, "Come, my sister. Let us experience the tent!"

Dotty uttered an expletive, removed Helene's arm, and headed off for their tent.

Mostyn shook his head, and walked out into the night. The wind was strong and blew a fine spray of stinging sand. He looked up into the sky. There were no clouds and the stars were bright, though somewhat obscured by the blowing sand. The moon had just risen and was hanging low in the eastern sky.

Mostyn looked around the tops of the dunes that surrounded the ruins on three sides. He could see the swirling sand dancing in the moonlight as though it were the raiment of ghosts. He turned and looked out towards the salt flat. Everything seemed calm out there. The crystals of salt glinted in the light of the moon.

He pursed his lips and filed the information away. From long experience, he knew there was the natural and the supernatural. The normal and the paranormal. And Mostyn had a hunch the wind they were experiencing wasn't natural or normal.

5

GREEN EYE

MOSTYN TOSSED and turned on his cot. The events of the day and evening were weighing on his mind. He listened. The wind had died down. At least that was good.

Sick of tossing and turning, he got off his cot, grabbed his clothes, got dressed, making sure to shake his boots to dislodge any newly resident spiders, and left the tent. A lizard scuttled away from the tent flap. Mostyn dropped his foot heavily on a camel spider, but missed, and watched it run off.

The night air was still hot, even though the time was after midnight, and his throat was parched due to the searingly dry air. He wandered over to the mess tent to get water, and, after drinking his fill, stepped back out to stand under the moonlit sky. Eerie shadows lay across the ruin and the edges of the camp.

He thought, *This is the atmosphere horror and suspense writers seek to achieve.*

Out by the salt flat, he saw Hal Neumeyer standing guard. On the other end of camp, Donovan White was walking slowly around the perimeter. He didn't envy them.

Mostyn looked up at the dunes. After a moment, he let his eyes run across the tops of the buildings, which, in the light of the moon, looked even more alien and bizarre than in the daytime. Only the sand had the look of something completely of this Earth.

He felt a certain unease, but he couldn't put his finger on it. Sure there was the city, but he'd experienced that disquieting feeling of things left behind by the Great Old Ones or their followers before, and this wasn't it.

Was it Salih and the fear he was manifesting? Or was it something else? Something niggling at his subconscious brought on by the evil of this place? Because for all of his words to Salih and the team, Mostyn felt a palpable evil lurking, waiting in the ruins. An evil that was different from that connected with the sycophants of the Great Old Ones.

He felt an underlying presence, like a foul odor that you can't find the source for, that permeated the stones of the buildings, the air, the sand. Which only reinforced his belief that ancient Iram was indeed a gate. A gate that allowed the unimaginably noxious and obscenely unnatural entities of another dimension to invade the world.

He gazed at the moonlit ruins. They seemed to taunt him, mock him, as if they were a living thing. He shook his head, told himself to get a grip, and retraced his steps to his tent. He shooed away several camel spiders trying to get in, and lifted the flap to enter. Drifting on the night air, for just a moment, Mostyn thought he heard a high-pitched piping. A piping that was mocking and taunting.

———

The sun had been up for a couple hours when the team assembled in the mess tent.

Mostyn had finally gotten some sleep. When he woke, he dressed, and took a ramble around the camp to make sure everything was okay. When he got to the mess tent, there was the usual haggling going on amongst the team members.

"Does anyone want to trade me anything for a vegetable crumbles with pasta packet?" Dotty called out.

Salih yelled, "I'll trade. I got the pork sausage."

Jones was going around collecting everything anyone didn't want.

Baker handed Mostyn Menu 20.

"Hey, thanks, Willie Lee."

"Don't mention it, Boss."

"You wouldn't happen to have an extra coffee in there, would you?"

"No, I don't. But I bet you can get one from Jones." Baker then leaned in close to his boss. "I noticed this morning that it looks like someone was pilfering MREs."

"How can you tell?"

"Two cases were opened and the vegetarian meals were gone."

Mostyn pursed his lips in thought, then said, "Monitor it and keep me posted."

"Will do."

Mostyn looked around, spotted Dotty and Helene, and walked to their table to join them. He gave each a kiss, sat, and dug into his hash browns with bacon.

"Oh, Mostyn Pierce, this is so exciting!" Helene took a bite of the First Strike Bar. Mostyn watched a range of expressions cross her face.

"Tastes like shit, right?" Dotty said.

"Oh, no," Helene replied. "It is chocolate."

Mostyn nearly spewed a mouthful of hash browns and Dotty rolled her eyes.

Jones came up to them. "Anything you don't want?"

"You have a coffee in your hoard, Jones?" Mostyn asked.

"Sure. What will you trade for it?"

Mostyn smiled. "Not giving you a crap work detail. How does that sound?"

Jones muttered something and tossed Mostyn an instant French vanilla cappuccino and moved on.

"That was not very nice, Mostyn Pierce."

Mostyn shrugged. "I got a coffee and Jones doesn't get a crap work detail."

"You pulled rank. Is that the saying?"

"That's the saying, Helene," Mostyn replied. "And yes, I did."

Doctor Lentz called out, "When everyone on my team is done eating, assemble outside. I'd like us to be at the work site by quarter after."

Helene finished her energy bar. "Goodbye, Mostyn Pierce. Are you coming, my sister?"

"In a minute," Dotty replied, and put the last spoonful of sausage in her mouth.

"Okay, my sister, I will see you outside." Helene kissed Mostyn, and left.

"Keep an eye on her, will you?" Mostyn asked Dotty.

"Why? Are you afraid she'll wig out seeing all the statues and stuff?"

"More along the lines of better safe than sorry."

"Okay, Mostyn, I'll keep an eye on her."

"Good. Thanks, Dot."

Dotty nodded, finished eating a packet of nuts, drank her

coffee, and put the First Strike Bar in her pocket. "You want the peanut butter and crackers?"

Mostyn shook his head, paused for a moment, and then held out his hand. "I'll give them to Jones. A peace offering."

Dotty laughed, and handed the packets to him. "Catch you later, Mr. Boss Man." She blew him a kiss and left.

Mostyn stood, noticed Doctor Hyde was collecting her team, and looked around for Jones. He spotted him talking to Baker, and walked over to join them.

Baker was saying, "Didn't your mother feed you when you were growing up?"

"Of course she did." Jones said.

Mostyn interrupted. "Here you go, Jones. And thanks for the coffee."

"Hey, thanks, Boss! I love these peanut butter and cracker packets."

"The two of you get going. I'll finish up here."

"Thanks, Mostyn," Baker said, and went outside with Jones.

Mostyn watched the remaining team members file out of the tent. All except for Salih.

"Give me a hand, Salih."

"Yes, Mr. Mostyn."

The two men secured the food and policed any trash they spotted. When they were done, Mostyn clapped Salih on the shoulder.

"Let's go back to the city center. I want to poke around in some of the other buildings there. And then in the afternoon, I'd like to take a look around the area. Okay with you?"

"Yes, sir."

The two men walked out to the small ATV, after Mostyn

picked up backpacks, weapons, lanterns, water, and a couple MRE packets.

He drove the ATV out to the opposite side of the square from where Lentz's team was working. The building he parked in front of was smaller than the Hall of the Great Old Ones, and was flanked by two buildings that were smaller yet.

"Let's take a look at the middle building first," Mostyn said.

He and Salih walked up the stairs that led to the portico with some difficulty, for they were constructed with the same dimensions as those of the Hall. When they reached the portico, they went straight to the central doors, and opened them with no difficulty.

"Follow me," Mostyn said, and entered the building, while turning on his electric lantern.

Compared with the rapidly rising temperature of the outside air, the dark interior of the building was relatively cool. Mostyn swept the brilliant beam of light from his lantern around the immense space. Like the Hall across the square, this building also had large windows positioned near the roof. Light filtered in through the openings, but as the building was in the shadow cast by the great dunes of sand, it was insufficient and the inside remained mostly dark.

Salih turned on his lamp, and together he and Mostyn played the powerful beams around the enormous chamber. The floor was made up of colored tiles, and on either side of the wide central aisle was a row of many huge columns. The area between the columns and the walls, seemed to form side aisles, but these were filled in with sand that had come in through the open windows.

The two men walked further into the darkness, swinging their lanterns from side to side.

"The building seems to be larger than I thought," Mostyn said. "Rather narrow and long."

"So it seems, Mr. Mostyn."

They continued walking down the central aisle, until they reached the end, where there was an extensive raised stage area, and, on the stage, there appeared to be an altar.

Mostyn mounted the steps to the top of the stage, with Salih following. The special agent walked along the front of the stage, playing the beam of intense light from his lamp to his right, then his left, and finally straight ahead. He repeated the pattern as he walked.

When Mostyn was satisfied that the front of the stage area was empty of anything significant, he turned his attention and his lamp to the large central altar, and directed Salih to do likewise.

The altar was massive and made of black stone. It was devoid of any markings. The top of the altar was a little over Mostyn's head.

"The people of this place must've truly been giants," he quipped.

"According to the Qur'an they were," Salih replied.

When Mostyn had circled around to the back of the altar, he felt cool air, almost cold coming from somewhere out of the blackness behind him. He turned around and began playing the lamp light back and forth across the floor, and slowly lifted the sweeping arcs until the light was at waist level.

"I think there's something back there, Salih."

Mostyn stepped to his right a dozen paces and moved forward. He shone the lamp straight ahead. "Yes, there's something there."

The chill air continued to flow out of the blackness that engulfed the rear of the building.

Mostyn lifted his lamp beam higher and higher. Something glinted in the light, and he stepped closer, Salih by his side. Mostyn made slow circles with the light and Salih screamed. For gleaming in the light of Mostyn's lamp was a huge green eye.

6

GOLD

TO SALIH'S CREDIT, he did not run. Saying something in Arabic, he slowly began backing up.

"Salih!" Mostyn yelled. "I need your light."

The young man stopped, took a deep breath, and replied, "Yes, sir." He stepped forward and turned his lamp onto the giant object.

Mostyn began moving around the enormous piece of stone, and Salih followed. They played the beams of light up and down, and from side to side.

"This appears to be a giant idol, and I'm guessing from the general shape, to be one of Tsathoggua," Mostyn said.

"I haven't heard of that one."

"He's big, mean, bad, and ugly."

"Worse than the others?"

"Some think so. Let me put it this way: you wouldn't want to meet it in a dark alley at night. Or in the daytime, come to think of it."

"Or a dark temple," Salih muttered.

Mostyn chuckled. "Or there, too. Thank your lucky stars this is just a great big hunk of rock."

They'd moved around the huge idol and were now behind it.

"I don't feel the cold draft," Salih said.

"I don't either. That means it must be coming from some opening in the front of this thing."

Mostyn and Salih circled around the other side of the hideous sculpture until they were standing in front of it.

"Yep," Mostyn said, "it's coming from somewhere ahead of us. There must be an opening, which probably leads to someplace below ground."

Mostyn started walking forward.

"Is it safe?" Salih asked.

"You mean the underground chamber?"

"Yes."

"Don't know. Probably as safe or as dangerous as anything else around here."

Mostyn forged ahead, with Salih in his wake. The closer he got, the stronger he felt the flow of cold air, and then the beam of his lamp picked up an open entrance, some ten feet high and about four feet wide.

"I think we found the source of our cool air," Mostyn said.

"It feels cold to me," Salih replied.

"Where are you from?"

"Texas."

"Gets doggone hot there."

"Yes, it does. Very hot. And humid."

Mostyn stood before the doorway, Salih next to him. The flow of air was steady and more than just a light breeze.

"Well, what do you think?" Mostyn said, thrusting his lantern into the opening.

"I don't think I like fieldwork."

Mostyn chuckled. "It does have its downside."

The lamp revealed a square room. There were various motifs painted on the walls. At first glance, they appeared to record the coming of the Great Old Ones and the founding of the city. Set into the far wall straight ahead of them was a door.

"Come on, Salih, I want to find out where this air is coming from."

Mostyn entered the room, Salih behind him. To his left, Mostyn noticed an alcove that he hadn't seen from the entrance. At the back of the alcove was an opening, and from it came the cool air.

"I wonder where this leads?" Mostyn said, more to himself than to his companion. He walked over to the opening, which was rectangular, a doorway without a door, and let his lamp illuminate the darkness. "Aha! Look at this, Salih, a staircase."

"And let me guess, it goes down."

"Right you are. Let's see how far down it goes."

"Do we have to?"

"Of course we have to. Our job is to go where no sane person has gone before. Didn't Bardon tell you that?"

"No."

"Sorry to be the one to have to break the good news to you. Come on."

Mostyn proceeded down the stairs, which appeared to be carved out of solid rock. The steps themselves were smooth. The walls and ceiling of the stairwell were roughhewn. The lamplight showed the steps disappearing into the Stygian blackness beyond the reach of the lamp's powerful beam.

"Do we have to go down there?" Salih asked. "I'm a translator. I should be with the others in case the Bedouins or the Saudis show up."

"Perhaps. However, I'm the mission commander and I decided you are with me. Now man up and let's go."

"Yes, sir."

"Those Bedouins must've made a deep impression on you, for you to be this skittish having grown up in America."

"They have survived for millennia in this wasteland. They know deep and hidden secrets. Yes, they made an impression."

Mostyn nodded and down the steps he went, Salih following. The steps seemed to go on forever. Even Mostyn, after a time, began to wonder if he wasn't being a tad foolish. Yet he pushed on and eventually the steps ended in a large antechamber.

He panned his lamp beam along the walls and ceiling, directing Salih to do likewise. The ceiling was bare stone. The walls, however, were painted with a variety of religious scenes. The antechamber was devoid of any furnishings or paraphernalia. Just a bare room.

In each of the walls, there was a door. Mostyn examined the one to his left. It was large and made of stone. He pushed on it and it grudgingly swung in. He stuck his lamp into the opening. The light revealed more steps going deeper into the earth.

"That's not my top choice to explore," Mostyn said. "Let's try door number two."

The door directly opposite the staircase they'd just come down was also made of stone. Mostyn pushed on it and it swung in. He shined the light from his lamp into the darkness and saw a long corridor, with wooden doors running the length of the passage on both sides.

Mostyn then turned to the final door. It was made of thick, heavy timbers and was ornately carved with religious imagery. He took hold of the handle and pushed. The door swung open, and Mostyn's lamp revealed a large room sumptuously furnished and richly decorated. He walked in, and Salih followed.

"What is this?" the young Arab-American asked.

"Offhand, I'd say it was the quarters of the high priest of Tsathoggua. And the corridor with all the doors was probably where the regular priests lived."

"And the stairs?"

"My guess is a burial crypt for the priests."

Salih played his lamp around. "There's a lot of gold here. Enough to make us fabulously wealthy. Especially with gold at thirteen to fourteen hundred dollars an ounce."

"I thought you were religious."

"I am."

"So what's this interest in gold? Isn't being rich against what most religions teach?"

"My parents are poor. They worked hard and saw everyone around them prosper. So they came to America with the hope that things would be different for their children. There's nothing wrong with money, or in this case gold. It is all in your intention as to what you want to do with it."

"Well, you're right: there is a lot of gold here. And as I said to you before, you don't want to be taking *any* of *this* gold. Good intention or not, nothing good will come from pocketing this stuff."

Salih was gazing at a solid gold toad-like effigy about the size of a softball.

Mostyn continued, "So put that thing down and take a picture of it for the record. In fact, let's take quite a few pictures for the record." And Mostyn took out his phone and busied himself photographing the murals on the wall, while Salih took pictures of the gold.

After some time had passed, Mostyn said, "Time to go. We'll grab some lunch, and then take a tour of the surrounding area."

"Yes, sir."

The two left the opulent chamber and began the long trek back up the staircase to the upper temple and the surface. As the light from their lamps faded, the door to the high priest's chamber silently swung closed.

7

RAIDERS

MOSTYN AND SALIH ate their lunch with Doctor Lentz's team, and while doing so, they described what they had found in the temple of Tsathoggua. Mostyn found it a bit strange that Salih's fear of the place seemed to evaporate when he talked about the gold. Doctor Lentz made a note of their findings and said he'd take a look himself.

When lunch was over, Mostyn and the young Arab-American drove the ATV back to camp, transferred to a Humvee, and took to the desert.

Around the ancient ruin Mostyn drove, taking careful notice of the terrain. That the salt flat had once been a lake or an inland sea looked obvious to him. Iram had been built in a large valley on the shores of that primordial body of water. Surrounding the valley, rising up from the lake, was higher terrain. It was difficult to determine how high the surrounding land was due to the fact it was now completely covered in sand. The dunes surrounding the ruin towered upwards of three hundred feet or more. They were like a ring of mountains surrounding the ancient ruin.

What Mostyn found difficult to imagine was the magnitude of the sandstorm that had uncovered the city, even though sand still filled in a great portion of the valley, including large sections of the ruin. There was an immense area that was now seeing the sun for the first time in thousands of years.

However, he thought it strange that the effect of the storm was peculiarly localized. Just this valley and nowhere else.

He drove the Humvee across the salt flat and swung into the dunes south of the city. According to the report from OUP intelligence, there were no roads, water wells, or oases within a hundred miles or more of the city's location.

So why, Mostyn thought, *is there that dust cloud on the horizon?*

He stopped the Humvee two hundred feet up the side of a sand dune. "What do you make of that, Salih?"

"Some kind of vehicle. Too much dust for camels."

Mostyn nodded, and grabbed a pair of binoculars. He trained them on the growing cloud of sand.

I don't think I like this, he thought. *I doubt it bodes well for us.*

"Here, Salih, take these and keep them trained on whatever it is that's out there. I'm going to see if I can't get us a bit higher."

He moved the Humvee about fifty feet further up the dune. "What do you see?" he asked.

"Some kind of vehicle."

Mostyn took the binoculars, adjusted them, and looked at the source of the sand and dust cloud. "Oh, this is not good. Not good at all."

"What is it, Mr. Mostyn?"

"Saudi M one-one-three."

"What is that?"

"An armored personnel carrier. And it's headed this way."

———

Mostyn drove back to the camp as if he was trying out for the Indy 500. He pulled into the place where the vehicles were parked and sent Salih to warn Lentz's team to hide, with instructions to return when the message to Lentz had been delivered. Mostyn himself went to where Doctor Hyde's team was working.

"NicAskill!" he yelled.

She came out from a building. "You rang, Boss?"

"We're going to get company very soon. Take Hyde and Monroe to the city center and find a place to hide."

"On it, Boss." NicAskill left to collect the two professors and take them to safety.

Hal Neumeyer came out of a building. "What's all the commotion about?"

"Visitors. Not the friendly kind. I want you to disable the vehicles and hide the radio. When you're done with that, help me hide as much of the supplies as we can."

"Gotcha, Boss."

While Neumeyer went about his task, Mostyn began moving water from the supply tent to one of the nearby buildings in the ruins. When Salih returned, Mostyn put him to work hiding food and water, and moved on to the weapons tent to hide as much ammunition as he could. Weapons without ammunition were pretty much worthless. Mostyn hoped the visitors would leave the weapons alone when they saw there was no ammunition for them.

When Neumeyer finished his task, Mostyn directed him to help Salih. The three men worked fast to hide as much of their supplies and ordinance as they could.

After a time, Mostyn heard the faint, labored drone of the M113's engine. "Okay, they're nearly here. Leave whatever's left, load up on weapons, and let's hide. Salih, you go back and hide with the others. Neumeyer, position yourself in that building." He pointed to where he wanted Neumeyer to go. "I'll be over there, across from you."

Neumeyer smiled. "And the Arabs will be in the middle."

Mostyn flashed a thumbs up.

———

The M113 rolled into the camp. Mostyn, who was on the second floor of a two-story building, watched through his binoculars as the thirteen Saudis exited the vehicle. Two were armed with sidearms, the other eleven with standard Saudi issued H&K G3 battle rifles. One of the men was directing the others to fan out and search the camp.

On the floor, next to Mostyn, was a walkie-talkie so he could communicate with Neumeyer, and hopefully Jones and NicAskill if they were in range, a sniper rifle, and an MP5 submachine gun. On his tactical belt, were his pistol, a couple knives, ammunition pouches, a garrote, and three grenades.

He watched the Saudis as they went through the camp. They appeared to be Border Patrol, from the insignias he saw on their uniforms. The question Mostyn asked himself was what were they doing here, hundreds of miles from any international border? The only answer he could come up with was that they weren't paying an official visit.

"Probably looking for stuff to loot and sell," he muttered. Which begged the question, how did they know he and his team were in this place to begin with? Either they were seen when they parachuted in, or there was a leak somewhere. The first was a hazard of any operation. The second possibility was far more dangerous.

The men returning from their search of the tents didn't appear to be happy campers, which made their commander a *very* unhappy camper.

"Good," Mostyn murmured. "Maybe now you'll go away and leave us alone."

He watched the commander send three men to the motor pool area. When the vehicles didn't start, Mostyn chuckled at the commander's reaction.

"That's one pissed off black marketer," he murmured.

However, when he watched them start maneuvering one of the trailers towards the armored personnel carrier, that's when he decided it was time for some fun and games.

He positioned the sniper rifle on the window ledge, pulled back the bolt and pushed it forward, chambering a round, and looked through the scope. He estimated the Saudis to be about seven hundred yards away. After a moment's thought, he adjusted his aim to allow for distance, the heat rising off the ground, and the light wind.

Mostyn squeezed the trigger and the rifle fired, the suppressor muffling the report and muzzle flash. He watched the bullet ping off the side of the trailer. The Saudi unit froze, looking for all the world like a scene in a wax museum.

He chambered another round and sent the bullet into the sand a couple feet from the commander. Suddenly there was a stream of rapid-fire Arabic and thirteen men were hugging the sand.

Now they'd be looking for him. He heard a rifle report. Neumeyer.

"Thanks, Hal," Mostyn murmured, and watched the Saudis attention move in the general direction of where Neumeyer was hiding.

After a minute or so of quiet, the Saudis were on the move. They quickly got into combat positions. Mostyn cursed. They weren't pulling out, they were preparing for a fight. Rifles began to bark and Mostyn watched two men get into the M113.

"Damn," he said, when one of them manned the machine gun on the vehicle.

Mostyn took aim and fired. The bullet was too low and hit the armor plate protecting the machine gunner.

The open turret swiveled around and the machine gunner sent a wild burst of gunfire in Mostyn's general direction, but nowhere near him.

Mostyn took careful aim. They didn't know where he was yet, but it was only a matter of time before they figured it out. He watched three Saudi soldiers begin moving in his general direction. Aim, take a breath, exhale part of it, hold, squeeze the trigger. The rifle fired. Through the hot desert air the bullet flew. Mostyn was aware of some shouting, something in Arabic, and then the sound of rifle fire, and the thunk of bullets as they slammed into the ancient bricks. At the same time, through the scope, he watched the machine gunner fly backwards as though an invisible fist had slugged him.

Time to move. He grabbed the rifle, and his other equipment, and ran down the steps to the ground floor of the building. He ran across the empty ancient street into another building, and up the stairs. The upper story walls of this building had collapsed, and Mostyn hit the floor, crawling to the edge.

The Saudis were falling back, and piling into the armored personnel carrier. In another minute the M113 was throwing up sand as it raced out of camp.

Crisis averted. However, Mostyn had a feeling they hadn't seen the last of those guys. And next time, they'd undoubtedly bring friends.

8

MALEVOLENT FINGERS

MOSTYN STOOD BEFORE HIS TEAM. They'd all been in the field, except for Salih, and had had their share of wrestling matches with the unknown. And with things that were ultimately far more dangerous than a bunch of Saudis looking to make a fast buck.

He said, "I believe these guys will be back, and they'll probably bring friends. They now know something is here."

"How did they know we were here in the first place?" Doctor Lentz asked.

Mostyn shrugged. "Who knows? Somebody in the Ministry of the Interior talked to someone in his family who's related to someone in the Border Patrol, who happens to have a tribal affiliation with someone else, who said, 'Check this out, we can make a fast buck.' And we get a visit. That's one scenario."

"Shouldn't we notify Bardon?" Jones asked.

"Did that," Mostyn replied. "We're to work as fast as we can and be as thorough as we can. Which means, Doctor Hyde, I want your team to explore the buildings around the central square with Doctor Lentz. White and Neumeyer, I want you two to watch the entrance to the city from the salt flat."

They both gave Mostyn a thumbs up in reply.

"I want everyone armed. You've all had training. Now's the time to put that training into practice. We need to be ready to meet whatever demons decide to come out of these dunes."

"I've heard about Ms. Dubreuil's ability to dematerialize things," Doctor Hyde said. "Can't she somehow cloak us from any prying eyes?"

All eyes turned to Helene, who had a puzzled look on her face. "What does *cloak* mean?" she asked.

There were a few titters in the group.

"A cloaking device like in *Star Trek*," Doctor Munroe said.

Helene's face was a blank.

Mostyn intervened. "No, Ms. Dubreuil does not have the ability to hide this site from spying eyes or from intruders. Sorry, Doctor Hyde."

"Why don't we get in touch with the Saudis?" Dotty Kemper asked.

"Bardon's concerned they'll want to send troops to protect us," Mostyn replied. "They don't know the real reason we're here and Bardon doesn't want them to know."

"Typical," Dotty said. "Protect everyone from knowing the truth while we get our asses shot off."

"It's our job," Mostyn replied. "We deal with the night-mares so that the people of this planet can get a good night's sleep, and see tomorrow."

The look on Dotty's face was one of pure disgust. Mostyn ignored it. He knew Dotty's moods. And knew them well.

"Do the rest of you have any questions?" he asked. When

he saw that there were none, he said, "Meeting's over. Get some supper."

Baker left to pick up a case of MREs for the evening meal, while White lit the propane hot plate and put the kettle on, in case anyone wanted a hot beverage. Jones made his way over to Mostyn.

"You know, Boss, we don't have enough personnel to establish an effective perimeter."

"I know."

"So what should we do?"

"There's not much we can do. As you pointed out, we're a little short on manpower."

"NicAskill could watch the eggheads, and I could take a Humvee out to watch for anyone coming."

"You could," Mostyn replied, and took a moment to consider Jones's idea. He shook his head. "No, Jones. I want you and NicAskill with the academics. I have no idea what we might uncover. If the gate is still open, or something opened it and that's why the city was uncovered, then we'll be in a bigger pile of hot steaming crap than any number of Arabs can dish out."

"But I thought all those Great Old Ones were already here and they're snoozing until someone or something wakes them up."

"All we know is that there are Great Old Ones here. We don't know if there are more on the other side waiting to come over or not."

"So better safe than sorry."

"Got it in one, Jones."

Baker returned with the MREs and everyone lined up to get their supper. Mostyn walked outside.

The moon was up and with it the wind had risen, which

picked up fine sand particles that turned the air to sandpaper. The pale ghostly glow illuminated the little whorls and tornadoes of sand that passed along the tops of the dunes and across the salt flat.

There was a beauty to the desolation and there was a feeling of terror. The Empty Quarter was an unforgiving place, with little drinkable water, no shade, and the relentless heat.

Then there's this place, this city, this gateway to realms of sheer terror and nightmare, Mostyn mused.

He thought of the uneasiness that niggled at the edges of his mind. The malevolent fingers that caressed and at times almost stilled his heart. The feeling of fearful dread that went beyond the unrelentingly harsh reality of the desert, a dread born out of the primal fears that lurked within his soul.

In his mind appeared the words, *My husband, where are you?*

Mostyn sent his thoughts to Helene, *I'm thinking, my precious one. I'll be there in a minute.*

Mostyn took a last look at the night and the ruined city of worshippers of the Great Old Ones. And in the heat of the night, he shivered.

9

SCREAM

MOSTYN ENTERED the mess tent and found Helene and Dotty, who were sitting with Doctors Maddy Hyde and Waldemar Lentz. He grabbed an MRE out of the box, chili with beans, along with a spoon. However, before he could step away, Baker stopped him.

"I'm willing to wager that our light-fingered vegetarian is Salih."

"What makes you say that, Willie Lee?"

"Saw him near the supply tent before supper. I stayed out of sight. He looked awfully guilty. So when he left, I checked, and sure enough a vegetarian MRE was missing out of a case I hadn't opened. He doesn't eat meat, a religious thing, right?"

"Not our meat, at any rate."

"Well, there you go."

"Thanks, Willie Lee. I'll talk to him. Maybe he's just hungry."

Baker patted his ample stomach, and said, "So am I. But you won't find any desserts missing."

"Got your point. Thanks." He walked over to the table

where Dotty and Helene were seated and took a seat between them.

"Fascinating temple you discovered, Mostyn," Lentz said. "I've never seen so many images of the Great Old Ones all in one place."

"They're positively hideous," Hyde said, by way of added commentary.

"You've seen them?" Mostyn asked.

"Pictures," she replied.

Mostyn nodded. "Just be glad you haven't seen the real thing. Pictures and statues are bad enough. With the real deal..." Mostyn shrugged. "You'd probably be a gibbering lunatic."

"I can see why," Hyde said.

"My people served them," Helene said. "Although their sleep has been for so long, most have forgotten them."

"You haven't," Lentz said.

"I pay them respect, but am a poor servant," she replied.

"As far as I'm concerned," Dotty said, "those things are just plain evil."

"Evil, or just don't give a damn where we're concerned," Mostyn countered.

"Evil, Mostyn, plain evil, and I don't care what you think."

"That's your opinion, Kemper. Doesn't make it so."

"If that's the case, Mostyn, why are you trying to stop them?" Dotty shot back. "Just let nature take its course."

Mostyn set his spoon down. "Because I happen to enjoy life and I don't care to have it prematurely cut short."

Helene, who'd been lost in thought, said, "I suppose that makes my people evil. Makes me evil."

Everyone at the table got quiet. After some time passed,

Lentz asked, with a bit of hesitation in his voice, "You don't want to exterminate us, do you?"

"Oh no, not at all. I love my new life with you." She looked at Mostyn. "And with my husband."

"You aren't evil," Mostyn said. "You left your people."

"Oh, good," Helene said, a big smile on her face. "I want to be like you. I want to be human."

"Be careful what you wish for," Hyde said. "Humans aren't perfect."

"Oh, I know that," Helene replied. "Nevertheless, I want to be human."

"You're close enough," Dotty said, and added, "*Homo*, just not *sapiens*."

"On a different note," Mostyn began, "has anyone seen Salih? I don't see him here."

"He was at the team meeting," Hyde said.

Lentz nodded. "Yes, he was there. Haven't seen him since; however, I wasn't looking for him."

"He might have gone to the tent. I'll check there," Mostyn said.

"Speaking of tents, that's where I'm headed," Maddy Hyde announced. "I'm tired. This heat is a killer." She got up, wished everyone a goodnight, and left.

"Not a bad idea," Lentz said. He stood, bid everyone "goodnight", and followed Doctor Hyde.

"Come to think of it," Dotty mused, "I don't recall seeing the Arab when we were hiding. Did you Helene?"

"No, I did not, my sister."

"Rather strange," Mostyn said. "Right now he's afraid of his own shadow, or so it seems. I find it hard to believe he went off by himself somewhere."

"Like you said, Mostyn, he's probably in your tent," Dotty said.

Mostyn nodded. "Probably."

Dotty stood. "Up early tomorrow. I'm hitting the hay. Goodnight, Pierce." She kissed his forehead. "You coming, Helene?"

"Yes, my sister." Helene stood, leaned down, kissed Mostyn's cheek, and left.

Mostyn finished his meal, got a paper cup of instant coffee, and walked to his tent. He looked inside. Empty.

A look of consternation appeared on Mostyn's face. *Where the hell could he be? This is not like him, not like him at all.*

He looked out over the camp. The night was dark. Only the moon cast an eerie, pale light. He turned around and looked at the ruins of Iram. Quiet. Deathly quiet. Only the wind and the sound of the fine sand pelting the tent fabric could be heard.

"I can't imagine you'd be in the city," Mostyn murmured. "You're scared to death of this place. Worse than Helene."

He shook his head, and started to enter the tent.

A scream ripped through the night. Mostyn ran around to the back of the tent. The side that faced the ruins.

Another scream ripped through the night and was suddenly cut off.

The city, Mostyn thought. *It's coming from somewhere in the city.*

He looked towards the ruins. Pitch black. The city looked as though a giant can of black paint had been poured over it. Not even the moonlight penetrated the blackness.

And for a moment, just a moment, Mostyn thought he saw an enormously gargantuan shadow, blacker than the night, rise up, and withdraw deeper into the Stygian blackness covering the ruins.

10

LOST AND FOUND

THERE WAS pandemonium in the camp. Mostyn yelled, "Order!", and when that didn't work, he fired his pistol into the air. The noise level dropped to a soft murmur.

"Baker, Kemper, Munroe, Hyde, Lentz, and Dubreuil, I want you to go to the mess tent and wait there. Baker and Kemper, make sure everyone is armed. Go! Now!"

To the remaining team members, he said, "Arm up and get flashlights. We're going to see if we can find out the cause of the scream."

"I can tell you that right now, Boss," NicAskill said. "It's Salih."

"I agree," Mostyn replied. "However, we need to confirm and discover what happened."

The special agents and the security detail drew their weapons, put on helmets with mounted lights, and grabbed flashlights.

When ready, Mostyn gave the signal and they moved slowly down the wide central avenue that led into the heart of the ancient city. White and Neumeyer were designated to check out the side streets as the team came to them.

The moon's pale white light cast sharp shadows, shadows that were stark and ominously obsidian.

Mostyn thought about what he'd seen or thought he'd seen over the city just after he'd heard the scream. It was as if a black hole had descended on the ancient ruin and prevented the moonlight from penetrating. And then there was the thing, the shadow, blacker than black. None of that bode well.

"Over here," Neumeyer yelled.

The team congregated where one of the side streets opened onto the central thoroughfare. There, some five feet in, was Salih, or more accurately what was left of him.

"Geez," Jones said, "looks like some wild animal ripped him apart."

"You don't actually believe that, Jonesy, do you?" NicAskill teased.

"Just sayin' how it *looks*."

"Good save, big guy," she replied.

"What was he doing here?" Neumeyer asked.

"And by himself," Mostyn added, stooping down to look at the mangled body. The face was oddly untouched. Mostyn involuntarily shuddered, for the face was contorted into a frozen image of abject terror. He tried to imagine what had happened. He stood and took in the scene.

Salih was lying on his back. If he'd been standing, he would've been facing the main thoroughfare. *Which means,* Mostyn thought, *he'd probably been on his way* out *of the side street when he encountered the mysterious killer.*

"Jones, NicAskill, you two take the buildings on that side of the street." He pointed to his right. "White, Neumeyer, you two take the ones on the left. Check the ground floor only. See if you notice anything disturbed or out of place."

The four took off and began searching the buildings. Mostyn walked straight down the narrow street until it disappeared into the sand. He panned the beam of his flashlight back and forth across the enormous pile of sand that buried this portion of the ruin. There was no evidence it had been disturbed.

Mostyn walked back to where his people were conducting the searches. He heard NicAskill call his name, and waved his flashlight to let her know where he was.

"You need to see this, Boss."

Mostyn walked to where she was standing, and entered what he assumed to be a house. There were furnishings present. In a corner, he saw Jones squatting.

"What do we have?" Mostyn asked.

Jones turned around. "The dirt floor in this corner looked like it had been dug up and then smoothed over. Nicky and I started digging, and we found gold objects."

"Shit," Mostyn said. He stooped down and looked at the pieces. There were five, four of which were small idols. One, though, was much larger; roughly the size of a softball.

"I know where these came from," Mostyn said. "The priest's chamber below the temple of Tsathoggua."

"He stole these?" Jones said.

"That's what it looks like," Mostyn replied.

"But, I mean, he was scared of this place," Jones said.

Mostyn nodded. "He was. However, his parents were poor. They grew up poor and emigrated to America when they got the chance, he told me, because they wanted their children to have a better life than they had. He also told me that one of the reasons, perhaps now that I think about it, the main reason, he accepted Bardon's offer and joined the OUP was because of the money. He had a duty to support his parents. And Bardon offered him a lot of money, which to a poor person was like giving him the password to Ali Baba's treasure cave."

"So what happened to him?" NicAskill asked.

Mostyn stood. "There is a thought among some of the practitioners of the arcane that sacred objects removed from their home, the place of worship, call out to the deity they are dedicated to and that deity, when it finds them, exacts judgement on the one who removed the objects."

"Kind of like the curse of King Tut," NicAskill said.

"Yes," Mostyn replied.

Jones stood. "And now this."

Mostyn nodded. "Salih, when he saw all that gold, must've overcome his fear of this place, took these objects, and buried them here. This house is, what, about four doors in from the main street?"

"Five," Jones said.

Mostyn nodded. "Close enough to camp so that he could easily come back and retrieve them."

"Until he ran into the owner," Jones said.

"Right," Mostyn agreed.

"I thought these things, the Great Old Ones, were sleeping," NicAskill said.

"They are," Mostyn said. "Apparently, though, they can be summoned. That is their spirit, so to speak. And that's what probably happened here. The objects, removed from where they belong, called out to Tsathoggua's spirit, and it answered them."

"What about us?" NicAskill asked.

"I don't know," Mostyn replied. "What I do know is this: we aren't taking these things with us. Let's go back to camp."

They left the house, called White and Neumeyer, explained the situation to them, and then the five returned to the camp.

On the way, Neumeyer asked about Salih's body.

"We'll bury him in the morning," Mostyn replied.

Back at the camp, Mostyn told the others what had happened. There were the appropriate utterances of condolence, and a few remarks about Salih's foolishness, but it was the look on Helene's face that had Mostyn worried. As everyone was heading off to their tent, he pulled her aside and sent his thoughts to her, asking what was troubling her.

She replied, *If the Lord Tsathoggua has been angered, then all the gods will be angry — and that does not bode well for us, my husband.*

11

DEMONS IN THE NIGHT

THE SUN HAD BEEN UP for about half an hour, when Mostyn, Jones, and Kemper walked into the ruins of Iram to bury the body of Salih ibn Adi. The only problem was the body was no longer where they had left it.

"What the hell?" Jones said. "This is the same street."

"And he was here," Kemper said, "because there's plenty of blood."

Mostyn walked around the large blood stain. "There are no drag marks, so where did the body go?"

"Beats me," Kemper replied.

"It's like, what, he just disappeared?" Jones said.

"Demons in the night," Mostyn quipped.

"What?" Jones and Kemper said together.

"Just a thought," Mostyn replied. "The master slays and then lets his minions feed."

"I'm not liking the sound of this," Jones said. "That means we have some uglies running around here now."

"Could be, Jones, could be," Mostyn said.

"Did that bastard cause us *more* problems?" Kemper spat.

"Don't know, Dot," Mostyn answered, "but I suppose anything is possible. And I think he was legitimate." Mostyn had a grin on his face.

"Shit," she said. "That damn religious nervous nellie is going to get us all killed and he isn't even here anymore so I can kill him. Double shit. Goddamn Arab."

"Dot," Mostyn said, his tone cautioning.

She glared at him, and after a moment or two, took a deep breath, and asked, "Are we done here?"

Mostyn touched her arm. "We're done. Let's go."

They walked back to camp and entered the mess tent. Baker was there handing out MREs.

"Wondered when you three would show up," he said.

"Problem is," Jones said, "some boogie man stole the body during the night."

"Really?" Baker replied

"Yep," Jones said. "Whaddya got for me, Baker?"

"How about Asian-style beef strips with veggies?"

"Sure. I'll take it." Jones took his MRE and went off to sit with NicAskill and the Special Forces guys.

Baker handed Dotty her breakfast packet.

"Tuna? Goddamn it, Baker. We've worked together how long and you give me tuna?

"I'll take it," Mostyn said.

Dotty looked at him, "Thanks, Pierce."

Mostyn kissed the tip of his index finger, and touched her lips. She kissed his fingertip and smiled.

Baker handed Dotty another MRE. "You know, Kemper, you're lucky you have Mostyn."

"I know," she replied.

Mostyn and Kemper found Helene, who was sitting with Doctors Hyde, Lentz, and Munroe, and sat with her and the academics. Dotty looked at her MRE and wrinkled her nose.

"You don't like your meal, my sister?"

Dotty shook her head. "Creamy Spinach Fettuccine. At least it's better than tuna."

Doctor Hyde said, "Too bad I've started on my Chicken Burrito Bowl, I'd have gladly traded."

Dotty smiled. "Thanks."

"Did you bury Salih?" Helene asked.

"No," Dotty answered, then added, "His body wasn't there."

"What do you mean his body wasn't there?" Munroe asked.

"Just that," Mostyn answered. "His body disappeared overnight."

"An animal made off with it?" Lentz asked.

Mostyn shook his head, chewed, and swallowed a chunk of tuna. "No drag marks. Do you have any idea what that means, Helene?"

"No, I do not, Mostyn Pierce."

"It means trouble," Baker said, as he joined them. "That kid woke something up, and now we're going to have to put it back to sleep."

"Wait one minute, Baker," Kemper said. "How the hell did you get pizza?"

Baker put on a big smile. "You want mess duty?" Then he took a big bite out of the pizza square.

"You didn't get tuna, Dot," Mostyn said.

With a scowl and a pout, Kemper focused her attention on her food.

"So what did that kid wake up?" Hyde asked.

Mostyn shrugged. "I was hoping Helene could help us out."

"I'm sorry, Mostyn Pierce. I do not know."

He waved away her apology. "That's okay. If something's been woken up, we'll find out soon enough and deal with it."

They finished eating while making small talk. When he was done, Mostyn excused himself, went over to where Jones was sitting, and pulled him aside.

"I don't know what we'll be encountering, but I want us ready," Mostyn said.

"Don't worry, Boss, I'll make sure we have something to meet whatever those sleepwalking bad boys try to throw at us."

"Good, Jones, I'll leave you to it."

Mostyn walked outside and made his way to the edge of the city. He felt a breeze blowing from somewhere further in the cluster of buildings. Sand swirled in eddies down the long central thoroughfare towards the camp. And the wind was cold. Icy cold. Then the ground began shaking.

12

THE HALL OF THE DEAD

"Ho, ho! What do we have here?" Doctor Waldemar Lentz rubbed his hands together in anticipation of discovering a great find.

The mysterious earth tremor that had occurred after breakfast caused part of the floor to buckle in the Hall of the Great Old Ones. After clearing away a portion of the sand and the floor tile, a staircase was revealed.

The rest of the team gathered around the opening. "Who's with me?" Lentz asked.

Doctor Maddy Hyde, hands on hips, said, "You aren't getting all the glory yourself, Walt."

Mostyn intervened. "We'll check this out together. We don't know how stable things are down there."

"Very true, Mostyn," Lentz said. "You're right, we need to take precautions."

Mostyn continued, "Doctor Lentz, Helene, and Jones, you three are with me. We'll take the initial look-see. Then the rest of you will follow on my signal, except White and Neumeyer. You two I want up here for backup in case we get in trouble down there."

"Gotcha," White confirmed.

"Does everyone's flashlight and walkie-talkie work?" Mostyn asked.

The team members checked their equipment and confirmed everything was in working order.

"Okay. I'll lead. Helene, you will follow first. Next, you, Doctor Lentz, and Jones, you're the rearguard."

"Gotcha, Boss," Jones said.

"Let's go," Mostyn ordered.

Down the stairs the four went, flashlights piercing the dusty inkiness.

Mostyn ran a hand along the wall. Roughhewn stone. *Must be cut out of the bedrock underlying all the sand,* he thought.

When the steps stopped, they emptied out into a chamber, a chamber large enough that their flashlights could not fully illuminate it. The lights picked up stone tables and designs painted on the walls.

Mostyn got on his walkie-talkie. "NicAskill, Baker, I want you two to bring down a couple high-powered lights so we can see what this place is. Munroe, Hyde, and Kemper, come on down. Mostyn out."

The three doctors entered the chamber several minutes later. Kemper flashed her light around. "They prepared the dead here for burial," she said.

"I agree," Maddy Hyde said.

"That means there must be a burial chamber somewhere nearby," Lentz added.

"Maybe, maybe not," Hyde countered.

"We haven't encountered a place of burial up on the surface," Lentz said.

"No, we haven't, Walt, but it might be buried under the sand," Hyde replied.

"Possible," was all Lentz said in return, and continued to examine the walls.

NicAskill and Baker arrived with the large lights, set them up and turned them on. The brilliant beams illuminated the chamber like the sun.

"Ah, that's better," Lentz said.

Baker took out his camera and began snapping pictures.

Munroe was examining a section of the wall. "I think I found it."

"Found what?" Hyde asked.

"Lentz's burial chamber."

The rest of the team gathered around as Munroe deciphered the pictographs. "Yes," he said at last. "A rough translation is, 'Enter here all you who have crossed over into the land of plenty, the land of bliss, the land of peace, for you are blessed by all of the gods forever and ever.'"

"Doesn't sound as though they feared the Great Old Ones," Lentz said.

"No," Helene said. "We served them and they provided for us."

Everyone looked at her.

Finally Hyde said, "But they're evil. How could your people worship them? That's the piece I still can't figure out."

"What is evil?" Helene replied.

"Well, evil is...," Hyde seemed at a loss for words.

"Evil is what you don't know or understand," Helene said. "Are we evil when we swat a mosquito, or a fly, or step on an ant on the sidewalk?"

Hyde waved away Helene's statement. "That's different. But these, these things, Cthulhu, Azathoth, Shub-Niggurath, they don't even conform to the laws of physics. They're abnormalities. Blasphemies of an insane and malignant creative force in whatever hellish dimension they came from."

"Is that what I am?" Helene said, her voice angry and defiant. "Because my people came with these 'blasphemies', as you call them, to this planet."

"Well, uh, no, no, *you* aren't," Hyde replied. "You're something they created. You aren't them."

"But I was in the loins of my ancestors when they came here with the ones you say are evil, the ones who ruled this planet before humans even existed. The very same ancestors you just said were created by evil beings."

Mostyn, knowing it wasn't a good thing to piss off Helene, interrupted. "We're here to explore, not debate. So let's explore. Doctor Munroe, can we open this door?"

"I don't see why not. I don't see any evidence of a spell binding it."

"Then let's open it," Mostyn said.

"I don't see a latch," Jones said, and he put his shoulder to the stone door, which swung open causing him to almost fall.

The flashlights illuminated a corridor, and the team walked the length of it before it terminated into a stairwell and a lift. The ropes on the lift had long ago rotted away, or been chewed by animals.

"They must've put the bodies on the lift and lowered them, rather than carry them down these steps," Lentz said.

Kemper agreed. "Makes sense," she said.

The team went down the steps, descending another twenty or thirty feet. The steps ended in a large chamber that disappeared beyond the limits of the flashlight beams.

Down the center of the chamber were two rows of sarcophagi, that eventually disappeared into the darkness.

Along each wall of the interminably long chamber, in innu-merable niches, were wooden coffins.

"The Hall of the Dead," Doctor Hyde said.

Doctor Munroe was motioning for people to get out of the way. "There's something written on the floor."

After half a minute, he translated the ancient text. "Peace and blessing to all who herein rest; and to the person who shall disturb one of these sleepers, may his soul be forever cursed."

Hyde and Kemper said together, "Typical."

"I wouldn't be so quick to brush off the curse," Mostyn said. "Remember Salih."

At the mention of the young translator's name, the team got quiet, and in the stillness, Helene's soft voice was heard to say, "We should leave. We have been warned."

13

DECISION

"THAT'S NONSENSE," Doctor Hyde said. "This is a repository of knowledge. We should take at least one of the bodies here back for study." She pointed to Helene. "We might just learn more about you."

"To disturb these bodies is not wise, Mostyn Pierce," Helene said.

"I agree with Maddy," Kemper said. "This is a chance of a lifetime. This city predates the beginnings of ancient Egypt by millennia."

"I'm still not sure we need to bother," Mostyn said.

"Are you nuts, Mostyn?" Kemper said. "We've gained untold knowledge of the past by studying the dead of ancient cultures. We need to take one of these coffins with us. Actually, we need to take several."

"I agree," Maddy Hyde said. "The more the better."

"You're awfully quiet, Doctor Lentz," Mostyn said.

"On the whole, I agree with my colleagues."

"See, Mostyn," Kemper said.

"However," Doctor Lentz continued, "we are dealing with

the Great Old Ones here. This is not a normal city of Earth. We aren't dealing with ancient humans in this place. We're essentially dealing with extra-dimensional beings, whether they look human or not."

Doctor Hyde threw her hands in the air. "Oh, for crying out loud."

"Of all the... I can't believe this," Dotty said.

"So what are you saying, Walt?" Mostyn asked.

Doctor Lentz shrugged. "Logically, I agree with Maddy and Dotty. But part of me agrees with Helene. We have been warned."

"Are we talking, like, the curse of King Tut here?" Jones asked.

"Sharp as a club, our Jonesy," NicAskill said.

"I'm just trying to clarify things, Ms. Brainiac," Jones shot back.

"Something like that, Jones," Mostyn said.

"But much worse," Helene added.

Jones turned to NicAskill. "See, I was right."

"I'm just messin' with you, Jones," NicAskill replied.

"Well, what's it going to be, Mostyn, science or superstition?" Dotty asked, her hands on her hips.

Mostyn was on the spot. He could pass the buck to Bardon. That was probably the wise choice. Let them be mad with Bardon. On the other hand, he was the mission leader. The decision was ultimately his, even if he did pass the buck to Bardon. Because if anything went wrong, he was the one in the field. Not Bardon.

He took a deep breath and exhaled. "We'll take a body back with us for study."

"Mostyn Pierce, this is not a good decision," Helene

cautioned. "Nothing good will come from the desecration of these dead."

"We're here to learn as much as we can while we can," Mostyn said.

Helene looked at the floor and shook her head, then in a soft voice she began chanting in K'n-yanian.

"What is she saying?" Doctor Hyde asked.

Dotty shook her head, Mostyn shrugged, and Richard Munroe said he didn't know the language.

"Well, I don't like it," Hyde said.

"You got what you wanted, Doctor," Mostyn said. "Now I suggest you get to work and pick a corpse."

While Hyde, Lentz, and Kemper discussed whether to open one of the sarcophagi, or take one of the coffins from the wall, Mostyn sent his thoughts to Helene.

What are you chanting? he asked.

A prayer for protection, my husband. Hopefully, some of us will be spared.

14

GAMBLE

J ONES GOT on the walkie-talkie and told Neumeyer and White to get rope from the camp, and that he was on his way to pick it up from them when they returned.

In the meantime, Hyde, Lentz, and Kemper discussed what they should open: one of the wooden coffins, or one of the stone sarcophagi. In the end, they decided on one of the sarcophagi. Because, as Doctor Hyde put it, "They were probably the important people."

After a bit, Jones returned with the rope and set it down near the entrance.

"Let's start by removing the lid," Doctor Hyde suggested. "It should just slide off."

Jones looked at the thick slab, a frown on his face. "Wouldn't it be easier for Ms. Stealth to just dematerialize whatever's inside and bring it out?"

Hyde's face brightened. "Sure it would."

She turned to Helene, but before she could say a word, Helene said, "I will not desecrate the dead."

Hyde turned to Mostyn. "Order her to bring the casket out."

Mostyn looked at Helene. "I will not do so, Mostyn Pierce. Send me back to K'n-yan. I would rather face the hideous death that awaits me there, than desecrate these dead."

"I guess you are going to have to get that casket out of there yourself, Doctor Hyde," Mostyn told her.

"All of this is going into my report to Doctor Bardon."

Mostyn shrugged. "Go ahead."

Hyde glowered at Mostyn for a moment and then turned her attention to removing the thick stone slab that formed the lid of the sarcophagus.

Even with all of the team members, except for Helene, pushing on the heavy stone lid of the chosen sarcophagus, it took quite a while and a fair amount of cursing before the large piece of stone was on the floor.

"Oh, my God!" Hyde exclaimed, when she looked inside.

The other team members joined her, adding the light from their head lamps, and saw the reason for her exclamation. Inside the stone chamber was a gold coffin that gleamed brightly in the light from the lamps. It was about eight feet long and three feet wide. At the head of the casket, a face had been shaped in the gold. The paint that colored the face was still bright after untold millennia and revealed a person who looked human. A person who displayed the hauteur of the privileged.

"We don't have the means to lift it out," NicAskill said.

"No, we don't," Hyde agreed. "We'll have to break down one of the sides and slide the coffin out that way."

"It would be a heck of a lot easier," Mostyn said, "to take one of the coffins along the walls."

"But look at the gold," Hyde replied. "This was someone of importance."

"Let me get pictures," Baker said, "before you start smashing stuff."

Hyde picked up the walkie-talkie and asked Neumeyer to bring sledge hammers and pry bars.

Jones headed back to the surface and NicAskill volunteered to help him bring down the equipment.

Baker snapped a picture, and said, "You know, Maddy, it was love of gold that got Salih killed. Maybe it would be best to take a wooden coffin."

"So you're a superstitious twat like your alien friend there," the archaeologist shot back.

Dotty said, "Willie Lee and Helene are not twats. Let's keep it professional here."

"Easy for you to say," Maddy replied. "You and the alien are screwing the team leader."

Mostyn intervened. "Doctor Hyde, I think you'd best apologize. Unless you want a desk job in some forgotten corner of some forgotten museum where you, as a forgotten person, will live out your days in obscurity."

Hyde glared at Mostyn and Mostyn glared back at her. They stood that way for what seemed like hours but was probably only a matter of seconds, before Maddy Hyde looked away, admitting defeat.

"I'm sorry," Hyde said. "You're right, Doctor Kemper, I was being unprofessional. I'm sorry, and I apologize for my behavior."

Baker walked over and gave the archaeologist a hug. "Just trying to keep you and the rest of us from being some demon's lunch."

Jones and NicAskill returned with a couple pry bars and a sledge hammer.

"This ought to get us going," Jones said, as he and NicAskill set the equipment on the floor.

NicAskill looked at everyone and asked, "Is everything all right here? Did Jonesy and I miss something?"

"Everything's fine," Mostyn replied. "You didn't miss anything important. Let's get to work."

Rather than smashing one of the sides, the archaeologists decided to use the pry bars to lift the coffin enough so that a rope could be passed under each end of it. The team would then lift the coffin out of the sarcophagus by pulling on the ropes and thereby preserve the coffin's stone home.

Helene continued refusing to help and to avoid further criticism, dematerialized, vanishing from her teammates's view.

Dotty shook her head, and Jones shrugged. Only Baker seemed to be sympathetic.

The team divided up, two persons on each of the four rope ends and began pulling to lift the coffin.

"God, this thing is heavy," Jones said through clenched teeth.

"I think we need a couple more guys on this," Munroe added.

Lentz nodded. "Yes, we could pass a third rope under the middle and have those two guards help us."

"Neumeyer and White," Mostyn said.

"Yes, them," Lentz confirmed. A sheepish grin spread across his face. "Not good with names. Sorry."

"Okay, people, let it down gently," Mostyn said. "I think you two gentlemen are right." He picked up the walkie-talkie, got hold of White and told him that he and Neumeyer were required down below.

When the two men reached the chamber, a rope was passed underneath the middle of the coffin, Neumeyer taking one end and White the other. With everyone pulling, the coffin was slowly lifted out of the sarcophagus. The gold casket was then shifted so it could rest on the top of the stone crypt's walls. Jones and White retrieved the wooden platform from the lift well and positioned it next to the sarcophagus so the coffin could be lowered onto it.

After more grunting, groaning, and straining, the casket was lowered onto the platform and then dragged to the lift shaft.

"Now we run the rope through the pulleys and haul it up," Jones said.

"How are we going to get it up the stairs?" Munroe asked.

"We'll have to manhaul it," Lentz answered.

"That's how I see it, Doc," Jones said in agreement.

Dotty shook her head. "This had better be worth it."

"You'll be the only forensic anthropologist to have studied a being that pre-dates humanity and comes from another dimension," Hyde said.

Dotty smiled. "There is that."

Throughout the day, the team dragged and manhauled the gold coffin up to the surface. By the time the sun was sitting low in the western sky, the coffin and the long dead body it contained was in a tent not far from the mess tent, resting on supports, so it wasn't sitting on the ground.

After supper, Mostyn found Helene in the tent kneeling on the ground next to the coffin.

"This was a mistake, Mostyn Pierce. We should not have disturbed the dead."

"They're dead, Helene. Those down below and this one here are nothing more than desiccated meat and bone."

"It is not the body we need to fear, Mostyn Pierce. It is the soul. The life force. That is what we've actually disturbed."

"So we are all going to end up like Salih?"

"Possibly. Those souls will cry out and if they wake the Old Ones, or rouse their sleeping spirits, then we may indeed join Salih in death. Why did you allow this?"

"Because studying this being will help us understand the Great Old Ones better. The knowledge, I hope, will allow us to defend ourselves whenever they wake up, or should a gate open and more of them attempt to enter our world."

Helene was quiet. After a time, Mostyn touched her arm. She looked at him.

"Is this what you call a gamble, Mostyn Pierce?"

"I suppose so, my precious. I suppose so."

"I hope the odds are in our favor."

15

THE FACE

THE NEXT MORNING, the beginning of day three, saw the team back in the center of the ruined city examining more of the temples surrounding the city center, except for Helene who had been delegated by Mostyn to guard the gold coffin.

Doctors Maddy Hyde, Waldemar Lentz, and Richard Munroe were examining a temple dedicated to Shub-Niggurath, while Dotty Kemper had returned to the Hall of the Dead to examine the contents of one of the wooden coffins from along the wall. Jones and White had carefully removed the ornate wooden box from its niche and set it on the floor. Mostyn was present mostly to satisfy his curiosity, although he had helped Dotty remove the coffin lid.

Inside the coffin was an intricately wrapped mummy, the wrappings being very dark brown to almost black in color.

"Are you going to unwrap it?" Mostyn asked.

"That's a long and arduous process and often results in damaging the body," Dotty replied.

"So are you?"

"I don't think so. The resin used on the cloth is fairly hard. I'd have to chip this away, rather than actually unwrap the body. Besides, physical unwrapping is actually outdated. X-rays and CT scans will let us virtually unwrap the body without actually doing so. The scans preserve the integrity of the dead person's body."

"I see." Since Baker was with the other scientists, Mostyn took a few pictures for the official records.

Dotty, magnifying glass in one hand and a scalpel in the other, asked, "Did Bardon say anything about the find?"

"Be careful."

"That sounds like him." Dotty poked and prodded the wrapped corpse. "I'm not an Egyptologist, but I'd say this body is pretty much identical to those of Egyptian mummies. I wonder if the Egyptians learned the practice from these people?"

"Good question," Mostyn replied.

The walkie-talkie crackled into life. "Come in Mostyn, this is Jones. Over."

"Yeah, Jones, what is it?"

"You better get topside. Something weird's happening."

"Roger that. Mostyn out."

"Come on, Dot. Let's go see what Iram is throwing at us this time."

"This is starting to creep me out."

"How so?"

"The weird stuff that's happening."

"It goes with the job, you know that. Unidentified Phenomena?"

"Yeah, right. I've done weird. But this degree of weird...?" She shook her head.

They climbed up the steps to the great hall and then

walked out into the city square where they saw the other team members.

Everyone was looking and pointing at the sky. The clouds were black and roiling. The wind was blowing out of the northeast. Along the tops of the dunes that were above the valley, the sand was being whipped up into gritty, coruscating sheets. A mist of sand was falling everywhere.

Mostyn and Kemper walked over to where the team members were clustered.

"When did this start?" Mostyn asked Jones.

"About five minutes before I got you on the walkie-talkie."

"Did anything set this off?"

Jones shrugged. "Don't know. Baker was photographing pictures on the walls. Munroe was working on translating something. The archaeologists were examining the altar area. Unless you two did something."

"Don't know what it would've been. Kemper was looking at a mummy and I was taking pictures of the thing."

"Maybe they don't like their pictures taken."

"Maybe, Jones. Maybe."

"Look!" Baker exclaimed. He pointed at the sky, and began taking pictures.

To the west of the city, a face was struggling to appear in the churning mass of atramentous clouds. The wind began blowing even more fiercely than before and the air was filled with millions of stinging grains of sand.

"I don't like the looks of this," Jones yelled, trying to make himself heard over the wind.

"Me, neither, Jones," Mostyn replied. "Let's get everyone inside one of these buildings."

"Any preference?"

"The Hall of the Great Old Ones."

Jones took charge of herding the academics and the others to the large temple.

"What about Helene?" Dotty yelled.

Mostyn got close to Dotty's ear. "I better get her."

"I'm going with you."

"You should stay here, Dot."

"Look, Mostyn, I may not like her, but the three of us are a team, thanks to Bardon. I'm going with you."

"Very well, then, let's go." Mostyn got Jones on the walkie-talkie and told him he and Dotty were going to get Helene. Jones wished them luck.

Mostyn and Kemper ran down the broad central thoroughfare towards the camp. Behind them, the face continued its struggle to become a coherent whole. Seemingly with a vengeance, the northeast wind hurled sand at them, abrading any bit of exposed skin. The sky continued to grow darker, giving the valley the feeling of dusk fading into night.

When they reached the camp, they ran to the tent containing the gold coffin. There they found Helene prostrated before the coffin.

"Helene, you have to leave with us!" Mostyn yelled.

Helene sat up from the prostration. "I'm praying for our safety, Mostyn Pierce."

"That's all well and good," Mostyn replied, "but the wind is increasing and you're not safe here."

"Look at the face on the coffin and look at the sky," Helene told him.

Mostyn and Kemper took a good look at the painted golden face and went outside the tent, turning to the west where the clouds were attempting to come together in the form of a human face. Dotty gasped and Mostyn's eyes grew large. For in the clouds, the face that was trying to become a coherent whole looked very much like the one on the coffin.

16

CIRCLES

MOSTYN AND KEMPER ran back into the tent. "What's going on, Helene?" Dotty asked.

"He is angry and his soul is attempting to return to this world."

"Do you know who he was?" Mostyn asked.

"I do not, Mostyn Pierce. He was someone who had great power. Perhaps a high priest, or what you call a sorcerer."

"What happens if he succeeds?" Dotty asked.

"I do not know, my sister. I do not think his return will be good for us."

Suddenly the wind stopped. All three ran out and looked at the sky. The clouds were rolling away and the sun was shining, bright and hot.

"So he gave up," Dotty said.

"For now, my sister. For now."

Mostyn via the walkie-talkie alerted Jones that the immediate crisis was over and everyone should get back to work.

"Do you think if we returned this guy's coffin to the crypt that he'd leave us alone?" Mostyn asked Helene.

"I do not know, Mostyn Pierce."

"I'm going back to work," Dotty said. "We only have two days left after today."

Mostyn absentmindedly nodded, and Dotty departed. His eyes swept the top of the giant ridge of sand encircling the ancient ruin. He then shifted his gaze to Iram itself.

Helene stood next to him. "What are you thinking, Mostyn Pierce?"

"Nothing definite. I just have a feeling and it's not good. I think we've woken something evil and it's coming this way."

———

Mostyn stood on the edge of the city square. On his walk from the camp, he turned over in his mind the events that had happened thus far. Something was niggling his mind. In some remote corner of his brain there was... What? Something, he didn't know what, trying to get his attention. Unfortunately, that corner was very dark and he had no idea what was jumping up and down, waving its arms at him.

He shrugged and turned his attention to the giant fountain that was before him. Surrounding the fountain were the temples. His eyes swept across the buildings. They formed a circle more than they did a square. The fountain was circular and the temple ring was more or less circular.

Was the city itself circular? he asked himself. *There was too much sand covering the periphery to know for sure — but what if it was?*

He knelt down and drew a circle in the sand. The fountain. Then he drew a circle around the circle. The temples. Then he drew a larger circle enclosing the other circles. The city.

"Don't disturb my circles," he muttered. "Archimedes. Syracuse falling to the Romans. What if...?"

He ran to the temple where Hyde, Lentz, and Munroe were working, and told everyone to follow him. He called Dotty on the walkie-talkie and told her to join everyone by the fountain.

When he had his team gathered together, Mostyn said, "I think I may have found the gate."

"Where is it?" Doctor Lentz asked.

"Right here," Mostyn replied.

"This was a fountain, Mostyn," Dotty said. "Isn't that right, Maddy?"

Doctor Hyde nodded and said, "Looks like one to me."

"So, Mostyn, if this fountain is a gate, what do you do, throw three coins into it to activate it?" Dotty asked, hands on hips.

Titters rippled through the group.

Mostyn gave her a sarcastic look. "Archimedes was a mathematician and an astronomer, among other things. He was killed during the siege of Syracuse. Supposedly his last words were, 'Don't disturb my circles.' The Roman soldier didn't understand what he meant and killed him."

"So? What does that have to do with anything?" Doctor Hyde asked, her tone clearly indicating she thought Mostyn was wasting their time.

"What if, as a last desperate effort to defeat the Romans, Archimedes was using his knowledge of math and astronomy to summon a Great Old One?"

"That's far-fetched, even for you, Mostyn," Dotty said.

"Look." Mostyn knelt and drew his circles again in the sand. "Everything in the city, all the energy, is focused towards the fountain. This isn't actually a fountain. It's like, it's like..." He paused, and then his face lit up. "It's like an antenna!"

Baker took pictures of the fountain out of force of habit. "Sounds pretty wild, Mostyn." He shrugged. "Then again, we've run into some pretty weird stuff over the years."

"So are you saying the energy from whatever rituals were performed in these temples was focused to this spot and then that energy was channeled to create, or attempt to create, an opening into another dimension?" Lentz asked.

"That's exactly what I'm saying, Doctor Lentz," Mostyn replied.

"If you're right, Mostyn, then all we have to do is destroy this fountain, or antenna, to close the gate," Munroe said.

Mostyn nodded. "Exactly."

"Easy enough to do," Jones said. "The only question is now, or before we leave?"

"I think before we leave," Mostyn answered. "That will allow us time to collect data and relay it to Bardon."

"I have plenty of pictures," Baker said. "I'll upload them this evening."

"Good, Willie Lee. Okay, everyone back to work. We're running out of time."

Mostyn walked back to camp and told Helene of his discovery.

"Perhaps you are right, Mostyn Pierce. I do not know. My people did not attempt to summon more gods. We tried to wake those already here. And then after time, much time, we basically forgot about the gods. Our religion became nothing more than rituals we performed because we had always done so."

"I'll confirm it all with Bardon, and then we'll go from there."

Helene ran her fingers along the gold casket. "Your circles, my love, will not stop *him*. And I think right now *he* is of greater concern than the gate."

17

THIEVES IN THE NIGHT

THE DAY HAD GONE WELL. Munroe had translated quite a few texts and Baker had photographed the originals. Lentz and Hyde explored and sketched the floor plans of the buildings around the city square, with Baker taking photographs.

Dotty decided, given the thousands of caskets in the underground crypt, to unwrap one of the mummies and gather as much data as she could. She was able to cut away most of the resin-soaked cloth from one of the bodies in order to examine the desiccated flesh. She took her own pictures, and made a voice recording on her phone as she proceeded.

Mostyn sent off a radio transmission outlining his idea regarding the gate to see if Bardon would confirm it, and to get the go ahead to destroy the antenna. For the remainder of the day, he'd split his time circulating amongst the work crews and checking on Helene.

The K'n-yanian stood guard over the gold coffin and offered up prayers, which she hoped would appease the disturbed souls.

The security personnel helped the professors and kept an eye out for any problems.

At supper, everyone was upbeat. Even Dotty ate her MRE without a complaint. Jones, Neumeyer, White, and NicAskill moved the tables so that the entire team could sit together, instead of in little groups.

Dotty held up a plastic bag. "These are amulets I found interspersed in the wrappings of the mummy I examined. This is just like what was practiced in ancient Egypt."

Doctor Waldemar Lentz held out his hand and asked if he could see them. Dotty passed the bag to him.

While Lentz was looking at the amulets, Doctor Maddy Hyde talked about the general design, construction, and decoration of the temple buildings.

Doctor Munroe butted in, interrupting Hyde's monologue, to talk about some of the texts he'd translated.

When Hyde tried to regain control of the conversation, Lentz derailed her with talk about the amulets.

Only Helene was quiet. Donovan White had volunteered to relieve her at guard duty so she could eat with the group.

Mostyn sent his thoughts to her asking what was wrong.

I am concerned, Mostyn Pierce.

This mission isn't any different than any other. They are all dangerous.

It is not that, Mostyn Pierce.

Then what is it?

It is the evil. No one is taking it seriously. The evil is active here and we have disturbed it.

I'm taking it seriously, and others are too. It's just that we have a mission and the mission comes first.

Even if we die?

Mostyn thought a moment before answering. Then said, *Yes, even if we die.*

Very well, Mostyn Pierce.

Mostyn knew Helene was not happy with his answer, but it was what the OUP did. Each mission stuck its finger in evil's eye and hoped to hell the monster didn't bite back.

Everyone was finished eating and was in the process of cleaning up, when the sound of gunfire ripped through the night air.

"Everybody down!" Mostyn yelled. "Crawl away if you can!" Then he pulled the plug for the lights and plunged the mess tent into darkness.

The gunfire was sporadic until a machine gun opened fire and turned the mess tent into Swiss cheese.

All Mostyn could think of was Dotty and Helene. Had they gotten away? He hoped so.

"Mostyn. Are you still here?" The voice was just above a whisper.

"What the hell are you doing here, Dot?"

"I could ask you the same question?"

The machine gun started up again turning something else into Swiss cheese.

Two men entered the partially collapsed mess tent, shining flashlight beams around. A beam of light landed on Dotty.

The men started talking excitedly in Arabic. Behind them Helene materialized, and plunged a knife into the neck of one of the men and then disappeared.

His partner cried out, "Ya Allah!", and knelt down next to his fallen comrade.

The machine gun, which had been silent, opened fire again. The soldier stood, pointed his rifle at Dotty, and Mostyn pulled the trigger twice on his pistol. The man dropped his rifle, staggered backwards, and fell to the ground. Dotty was on him in a flash and plunged her knife into his voice box hard enough that it went through his spine.

Mostyn was on his feet. "Come on, Dot." He took one of the rifles, and tossed the other one to her.

"Helene, are you here?" Dotty asked, her voice just above a whisper.

The tall, dark haired K'n-yanian materialized before them.

"Can you get us out of here?" Mostyn asked.

"Yes, of course, Mostyn Pierce."

And the three of them disappeared.

In their dematerialized state, Mostyn led the women to the supply tent. There he picked out some additional weapons, and plastic explosives. All of which Helene dematerialized. The trio then left the tent and moved off a ways so Mostyn could see what was going on.

Parked on the edge of the camp was an M35, or what was commonly referred to as a "deuce and a half", a large US military cargo truck. Although, this one had Saudi military markings. Also parked on the edge of the camp was the armored personnel carrier.

So our Saudi border guard black marketers are back, Mostyn thought.

Off to one side he saw Doctors Hyde, Lentz, and Munroe. Then he saw a soldier shove Willie Lee Baker into a kneeling position with the professors.

Where are Jones, NicAskill, Neumeyer, and White? Mostyn asked himself.

His eyes searched the compound, but he saw little in the dark.

Several of the Arabs were excited, and Mostyn saw why.

They'd found the tent with the gold casket. In a moment, the tent was crowded.

Mostyn positioned himself and lay prone on the ground. Helene was next to him and Dotty was next to her. He then told Helene to make him visible.

He aimed, squeezed the trigger on the rifle, and watched one of the soldiers fall.

There was pandemonium amongst the Saudis as they searched the area looking for where the shot had come from.

"Invisible time and let's move," Mostyn said.

Helene dematerialized Mostyn and the three of them moved to the armored personnel carrier. On the side of the vehicle that was facing away from the camp, Mostyn had Helene rematerialize him. He placed the plastic explosives in the caterpillar track, and stuck in a fuse.

"Okay, Helene, invisible time again." And Mostyn vanished from sight.

The three moved near to where the two Saudis were standing guard over their captives. They were talking and pointing to the tent where their compatriots were gathered. With no more shots having been fired, the soldiers had gone back to ogling the gold casket.

Mostyn, satisfied his people were okay, moved off towards the city, with Helene and Dotty. Standing in the shadow of a building, Helene once again made Mostyn visible. He brought up an app on his phone, pressed a few virtual buttons and keys, and then pressed a large red virtual button.

There was an explosion. Mostyn smiled. *That ought to take care of that armored personnel carrier*, he thought. *With only one track, it won't be moving any time soon.*

Mostyn once again told Helene to dematerialize him, while

they watched the Saudis yelling and firing random shots at the dunes.

The guards got Baker and the professors to their feet. They made sure their hands were tied behind their backs, and then shepherded their prisoners to the armored personnel carrier. While damaged, and not able to move, the vehicle was still intact.

After opening the doors, the guards shoved their prisoners into the vehicle. The doors were closed and secured. The guards then joined their comrades, who had once again settled down when there were no more explosions, and helped them carry the gold casket to the deuce and a half.

The wind sprang up, whipping up great whorls of sand. Mostyn watched dark clouds blow in and obscure the moon. Gunfire erupted from the tops of the dunes. Two of the Saudi border guards dropped. The remaining men let go of the casket, and returned fire in a wild panic.

In his mind, Mostyn heard Helene. *Look, Mostyn Pierce. He has returned.*

Mostyn followed Helene's gaze. There in the clouds, illuminated by lightning flashes, was the face of the man in the gold casket. This time, the face was fully formed.

The shooters on the dunes made quick work of the panic-stricken border guards. Mostyn watched the last guard run off into the night. He also watched the Bedouins appear and converge on the camp. Near as he could tell, there were maybe two dozen of them. They came into the camp on camels and on foot.

One of them began barking orders. It was clear to Mostyn the Bedouins wanted the gold casket for themselves, and had just eliminated the middleman. It was also obvious they thought the sandstorm was your everyday ordinary sand blowing in the wind.

The Bedouins put the casket in the back of the deuce and a half, two got into the vehicle, and in a moment the engine roared into life and smoke belched from the exhaust pipe.

One of the Bedouins started screaming and pointed. Mostyn looked back towards the city. The face had grown an enormous body, and the apparition took a giant-sized step towards the camp, and then another.

The Bedouins were screaming, shouting, and yelling. A couple fired their rifles at the cloud man. Another giant step, followed by yet another. The camels bolted, men were running, and the truck driver, putting the truck in gear, promptly stalled the thing.

The mouth on the giant face opened and began speaking in a language that Mostyn guessed hadn't been heard for many millennia.

He watched the giant foot lift and then descend on the camp and the Bedouins. The only sound was that of the roaring wind. The cloud man dissipated and the wind stopped, leaving the ancient ruin and the valley in silence.

Mostyn, Dotty, and Helene reappeared.

"He has regained his powers and has reached out from the spirit world to this world," Helene said.

They walked to the armored personnel carrier and Mostyn removed the plastic tie that had secured the rear doors, and released his people.

"What happened?" Baker asked.

Mostyn turned and looked towards the camp. "Apparently the man in the gold casket never heard of the saying, 'Vengeance is mine, saith the Lord.' Because he just exacted some, and I bet what we'll find ain't pretty."

18

NOTHING BUT SAND

BREAKFAST WAS UNUSUALLY QUIET. In surveying the camp the night before after everything had more or less returned to normal, Mostyn had found the body of Donovan White. He'd been shot when the renegade border guards attacked the camp.

Lined up on the edge of the salt flat were the bodies of ten soldiers, and thirteen Bedouins. The Bedouins had been smashed flat, as if a giant had stepped on them.

Jones had quipped that maybe they should just bury them in place, but Mostyn said no. Which meant they had to dig the flattened corpses out of the sand, and the two in the truck had to be pried off the seats.

When the attack came, Jones, NicAskill, and Neumeyer had been able to fall back into the ruins, and had been planning a counterattack when the Bedouins made their attack. However, when the three saw the cloud man rise up out of the center of the city, they decided to let nature take its course.

Aside from White, the next casualty of importance was the

radio. Several bullets had turned the piece of equipment into trash.

There were, of course, protocols in place should Sumer Base stop getting transmissions from the team. However Mostyn and his team weren't entirely without options. There was the portable cell phone tower that used the communication satellite system and there was the emergency OUP satellite phone, which Jones used after the attack in an attempt to reach Sumer Base.

After several calls failed to go through, Jones announced that the satellite must be out of position.

Mostyn nodded and said to the team, "For the time being we're on our own. At least until Sumer Base has decided we've been out of contact too long."

"What I'd like to know," Doctor Hyde asked, "is why we're still here. Why didn't that apparition wipe us out?"

"Maybe he's saving the best for last," Jones joked.

"And maybe there's a perfectly good explanation for all of this without resorting to the supernatural," Hyde replied.

"Perhaps," Mostyn said. "However, now's not the time to debate this. I think we're in danger and we need to proceed accordingly. End of discussion."

The morning meal proceeded in silence after that, and when it was over, the gold casket was put back in the tent on its supports. NicAskill doused the bodies with fuel and set them on fire, after which the team returned to the city center to continue gathering information.

Mostyn remained in camp to keep an eye on things. He sent Helene to join the rest of the team.

Jones had orders to place explosive charges around the fountain, which, when detonated, would hopefully destroy the structure and prevent the gate from being reopened. That was Mostyn's greatest concern at this point. He didn't think Iram's appearance was the result of an act of nature. More and more, it was beginning to look like an act of the supernatural.

Mostyn looked over the armored personnel carrier. With only one track, it was useless. He decided to strip everything out of it. Given what they were up against, the machine gun and ammunition alone were worth their weight in gold. There was also water, food, and ammunition for the rifles.

On the other hand, the deuce and a half might come in handy. He had thought of destroying it, but decided to hold off in case his team needed it.

He got in one of the Humvees and drove out half a mile from camp. There was nothing to be seen but sand dune after sand dune, the bright blue sky, and the burning hot sun. Behind him smoke rose from the burning bodies. Otherwise things were as they had been for millennia.

The light breeze picked up and the wind swirled sand into miniature tornadoes that ran along the tops of the dunes and then disappeared.

Out to the west, Mostyn noticed the horizon looked very dark.

"Now what the hell is coming our way?" he muttered, and lifted binoculars to his eyes, adding, "Can't be anything good."

Through the binoculars he studied the western skyline and concluded a sandstorm was heading their way.

He got on the walkie-talkie and radioed Jones. When he answered, Mostyn said, "Looks like the mother of all sandstorms is heading our way. Find shelter for everyone immediately."

"Roger, Boss. Out."

Mostyn continued to study the storm and after several minutes said out loud, "It's moving fast. I better pick up supplies and join the others."

He drove the Humvee back to camp, noticing the wind was already getting stronger. He loaded the vehicle with food, water, toilet paper, a propane hot plate, shovels, lanterns, and spare batteries.

The wall of inky clouds was close and getting closer by the minute. He got in the Humvee and drove to the central square, confirming with Jones on the way, by means of the walkie-talkie, that the team was in the Hall of the Great Old Ones.

When Mostyn parked by the steps, Jones and Neumeyer were there to help carry in the provisions and equipment.

"You brought enough grub to last us a week," Jones said.

"If the storm's as bad as the sky looks," Mostyn pointed to the swirling black clouds racing towards them, "we might be buried up to our asses in sand. Best be prepared."

Jones had parked everyone up on the stage area by the altar, and Mostyn thought that was good, as it was out of the direct path of the open windows.

Mostyn addressed the team. "Listen up, people. We have one heck of a storm blowing in."

Maddy Hyde interrupted. "Is this a normal storm, or something supernatural?"

"I don't know," Mostyn replied. "I can only tell you I hope it's normal."

"You brought a lot of food and water," Doctor Richard Munroe observed.

Jones piped up. "Better safe than sorry, Doc."

Before Mostyn had a chance to speak, the sunlight vanished and the wind struck in all its howling fury. Sand blew into the hall from the open windows, making its way to where the team had congregated.

"Cover your nose and mouth," Mostyn yelled. "Let's circle up!"

Retreating to the corner furthest away from the sand blowing into the hall, the team hunkered down, forming a circle around the supplies. For over two hours they listened to the wild howling of the wind before it gradually subsided and the sun was again visible.

Mostyn stood and walked to the edge of the stage area. He stood there and surveyed the interior of the hall. Sand had filled in the western half of the building and only the tops of the statues were visible. The sand sloped from the windows on the west to the feet of the statues on the eastern half of the temple.

"This isn't looking too good. Is it, Boss?" Jones said, standing next to Mostyn.

"At first glance, no, it doesn't, Jones. Doesn't look good at all."

The rest of the team joined Mostyn and Jones.

Looking at the large doors at the far end of the temple, Mostyn said, "Jones, Neumeyer, check the doors and see if you can get them opened."

"On it, Boss," Jones replied, and grabbed two shovels out of the pile of equipment Mostyn had brought from the camp.

The two men slogged across the sand covered floor until they reached the giant doors at the front of the temple. Mostyn watched Jones shake his head, and continued watching as the two men began shoveling sand away from the doors. After some minutes, they began tugging at one of them until they were able to force it open.

What Mostyn saw wasn't encouraging. He crossed his

fingers while Jones and Neumeyer worked on opening the other large door. When at last the men pushed the door open, Jones looked back at Mostyn and shook his head.

Except for a strip of bright blue sky at the very top of the enormous opening, there was nothing but sand.

19

GUM

MOSTYN LOOKED at the wall of sand blocking the Cyclopean doorway. He took a deep breath and exhaled.

He turned to Helene. "Can you take us through that?"

"I can try, Mostyn Pierce. If it is very thick, I don't think so."

"Give it a go and see if you can get through."

"I will try, my husband."

Helene dematerialized. Jones and Neumeyer had already started digging in an attempt to make a path out of the temple. Mostyn and the others watched as first a trickle and then an avalanche of sand cascaded down from above and buried the two men.

Mostyn swore and yelled, "Come on! We have to dig them out!"

The team surged forward, and slogged their way through the sand covering the floor towards the doorway. However, before Mostyn and the others had reached their destination, first Jones, next Neumeyer, and finally a smiling Helene Dubreuil appeared. She waved, and then vanished.

NicAskill reached the two men first. She threw her arms around Jones and kissed him. Mostyn was next. He shook Neumeyer's hand and asked if he was all right.

"I'm fine, sir. Uh, don't I get a kiss?" Neumeyer said, a smile stretched across face.

"Sure, Hal, why not? Pucker up."

The smile faded. "Uh, that's okay, sir. I'll settle for the handshake."

"Good. Because I'm not kissing your ugly mug." Mostyn slapped him on the back. "Glad you're okay, Hal."

The rest of the team arrived and congratulated the men on their escape from the cave-in.

Hands on her hips, Dotty craned her neck back to take in the pile of sand blocking the exit. "Sure hope Helene can beam us out of here," she said.

Helene appeared. "I am sorry, Mostyn Pierce, the sand is too deep."

Dotty said, "Shit", and Mostyn sighed.

"Listen up, people. There's no magic pass to getting out of here," Mostyn informed his team. "Roll up your sleeves and let's start digging."

———

Throughout the day and into the night the team dug sand. The only breaks Mostyn allowed were forty-five minutes for the noon meal and another forty-five for supper. Because there were only the two shovels, most of the digging was done by hand or with the aid of a few clay pots and bowls that were found in the temple.

Dotty and Maddy Hyde commiserated together on the loss of access to the underground Hall of the Dead. The entrance lay under tons of sand on the west side of the building. Waldemar Lentz was more philosophical about the loss.

"We know it's there," he said. "We have one of the caskets, and you, Doctor Kemper, were able to examine one of the mummies. And, when we get out of here, we'll have plenty of other things to study."

"And if this place is still around after we leave," Baker added, "you all can come back and do a little excavating."

Lentz chuckled. "There is that, Mr. Baker. There is that."

Once, in the afternoon, they heard a helicopter circling the area. In the end, it didn't land and flew off. The disappointment was palpable.

Mostyn, concerned about draining the batteries for their flashlights, called a halt to the digging a couple hours after sunset. With the light from just one flashlight, the team huddled together on the sand by the doors.

To lighten everyone's spirits, Neumeyer got the team singing camp songs. Helene was excited.

"Oooh, this is a new experience," she declared, and sang the new songs with gusto.

When the team had sung all of the songs they knew, Mostyn announced lights out and everyone curled up on the sand. He took the first watch.

A bit of moonlight filtered in from the widening gap at the top of the mound of sand barricading their exit.

The night was quiet. Mostyn thought too quiet. There wasn't even a breath of wind. He wondered if the demons in the dunes would be able to get at them.

Can they get in, if we can't get out? He asked himself. He didn't attempt an answer. Some things were best left unanswered.

———

Daylight streamed in from the windows on the east. Neumeyer, who had the last watch, went around and nudged everyone awake, making comments such as "Rise and shine, beautiful" (said to NicAskill), or "Get up, you lazy butt" (said to Jones).

Breakfast was a subdued affair, everyone at some point spending a few moments gazing at the mound of sand blocking the doorway.

Mostyn finished his beef stew, and coffee. "Okay people, finish up and let's get to work. The day's a wasting."

A murmur of grumbling rippled through the group. Jones stood. "Come on. You heard the man. Drill ye tarriers, drill. Didn't we sing that last night?"

"Blow it out your ass, Jones," Dotty called out.

"That's the spirit, Kemper," he shot back. "Now put that attitude to digging."

Dotty flipped him the bird and got to her feet, the others following suit. And the digging commenced.

NicAskill had only been digging a few minutes when she stopped. "Hey, everybody, do you hear that?"

Everyone stopped working and listened.

"A helicopter," Doctor Richard Munroe said.

"I hope this time they stop," Doctor Maddy Hyde added.

The whump-whump of the rotors gradually got closer.

"They're circling," Jones said.

"Maybe looking for a place to land," Dotty added, her voice filled with hope.

"I hope it's one of ours," Maddy Hyde said.

"It's not Russian," Jones told her.

"They're leaving," Dotty said.

"No, they're just flying off a bit," NicAskill corrected.

The sound of the rotors faded, but didn't disappear. After a moment the sound changed again.

Jones punched the air. "They landed!"

Everyone waited. Minutes seemed like days. Then a voice, amplified by a bullhorn, began calling their names.

Mostyn took his pistol out of its holster and fired two rounds into the sand that was blocking their way out.

"If that's you, Mostyn, or any of the team, fire another round."

Mostyn did so.

"Gotcha. There is a lot of sand out here. Get as far away from the doorway as you can. We're going to blast you out."

"You heard the man," Mostyn said. "Let's go!"

The team moved back to the altar area and waited. When the explosion came, the sound was muffled, but the blast did the trick. The pile collapsed, leaving a big enough opening for the team to get through.

Mostyn and his people moved forward, as half a dozen OUP Special Forces agents entered the temple.

A tall lanky man called out, "I don't see you for five years, Mostyn, and I have to save your ass *again* when I do."

Mostyn called back, "Stuff it up your backside, Gum. How the hell are you?"

"Fine, Mostyn, fine."

The two men met in the middle of the great hall, shook hands, and gave each other a backslapping hug.

Mostyn turned to his team. "Everyone, this is Captain Marion Mitchell Montgomery. Known to friends and enemies alike as Gum."

"That's *Captain* Gum to you, you sad sack," Montgomery said, as he gave Mostyn a playful shove. To the rest of

Mostyn's team he said, "Follow us and we'll get y'all back home."

Mostyn and his team followed Captain Montgomery and his people out into the open sunshine. The first thing that struck Mostyn was that the mega-storm had pretty much buried the city of Iram west of the central square. The Humvee Mostyn had driven to the temple before the storm was buried up to the top of the engine compartment in the golden sand.

"I saw the pictures of this place when the storm uncovered it," Montgomery said. "That storm you experienced must've been a doozy."

Mostyn nodded. "It was."

"Your camp's a mess," Montgomery said. "I'll call in another chopper, so we can get you all home."

There was the crack of a rifle, and a puff of sand from the bullet's impact just a foot in front of Mostyn.

20

BEDOUINS

THE CRACK of rifles and the zing and thud of bullets filled the air.

"Cover!" Montgomery yelled.

Mostyn hit the ground and felt a bullet whiz above him. *That was close,* he thought, and began to low crawl towards the nearest building.

Bullets were everywhere. On the edge of his consciousness he heard the helicopter power up. Somebody cried out.

Damn, Mostyn thought, *someone's hit.*

He got up to run into the building and everything changed. The world got fuzzy and he saw Helene and Dotty. They were holding hands and Helene had her other hand extended to him. He reached out and took it.

Come, Mostyn Pierce, he heard in his mind. *Let us get to safety.*

As if far away, Mostyn heard the machine gun on the helicopter open fire.

Mostyn, Helene, and Dotty reached a building and went inside. Rematerialized, Mostyn heard the sound of battle loud and clear. He wasn't sure where the enemy was, but figured they were far enough away that his pistol was next to worthless.

The helicopter, though, was making up for any weapons deficiency he or his people might have.

He heard the crack of rifles and hoped Montgomery's people were getting in a few licks on whoever had ambushed them.

"It's a good thing Helene rescued me when she did," Dotty said. "I was pinned down in the open. Who the hell are those people?"

"Don't know, Dot," Mostyn replied.

"Listen," Helene said.

Dotty bent her head. "It's quiet."

Mostyn slowly made his way outside. Montgomery's people were on the street, rifles pointed up towards the dunes surrounding the ruins. He turned and motioned for Dotty and Helene to join him. He heard his name, looked around, and saw Montgomery walking towards him.

"Who the hell was that, Mostyn?"

"Bedouins, is my guess," Mostyn replied.

"Hit two of my people. Thank God for body armor. What about your people?"

Mostyn looked around and began counting. "Looks like I'm short two… No, wait, there they are. All accounted for."

"Let's get to the chopper and at least get the civilians out of here."

"Sounds like a plan, Gum."

The party of sixteen made their way back to the camp, where the helicopter had landed after turning back the attack, and was waiting for them. Upon entering, Mostyn called his team together. "Captain Montgomery and I have decided to send back everyone who isn't a Special Agent or Special Forces Agent."

"Now wait one minute, Mostyn," Dotty began.

Doctor Hyde interrupted. "We need to be here to oversee the loading of the casket."

"It's exceedingly old," Doctor Lentz added.

"Sorry," Mostyn said. "We just weathered one attack and another could come at any moment. We need to leave here pronto."

"I'm not going," Hyde said.

"I'm not either," Dotty added.

"This isn't a democracy," Mostyn countered.

Montgomery came up to Mostyn. "We have a problem and those people need to leave now."

"What prob...?" Mostyn didn't finish his sentence. One look at the tops of the dunes told him what the problem was. The Bedouins were back, and there were hundreds of them.

21

NOTHING GOOD

"Now!" Mostyn yelled. "Get in the chopper, now!"

Gunfire poured down from the dunes and from across the salt flat. The target was the helicopter. In a matter of minutes, the intense fusillade had damaged the engine and rendered the aircraft inoperable. Miraculously, the pilot and co-pilot were not injured.

Once smoke started billowing from the helicopter, the gunfire stopped.

"They obviously want to keep us here," Montgomery said.

Mostyn nodded. "Looks like it. The question is, why?"

Montgomery clapped Mostyn on the shoulder. "Well, Special Agent in Charge I think that question's for you to answer. I'm just here to save your ass."

"So how do you propose to do that, Captain? There's a whole hell of a lot more of them than there are of us."

"You just leave that to me, Buddy. Now, what do you have of importance here?"

"The gold casket. That's it, of archaeological value. Otherwise, there's our equipment, or what's left of it."

"Radio?"

Mostyn shook his head. "Although we do have the sat phone setup."

"Okay, that might work. Hopefully the radio in the chopper still works. Let's check your weapons. See if there are some goodies we can use."

Mostyn and Montgomery walked over to the half-down supply tent. On the way Montgomery said, "Rather odd for those Bedouins to just sit there baking in the sun. Don't you think?"

Mostyn nodded. "I do. But they aren't shooting at us, so let's make hay while we can."

At the tent, the two men replaced some of the poles and took a look at what was still stockpiled there. They were joined by Jones, NicAskill, and Neumeyer, in addition to Lieutenant Scarlett Clifton and Sergeant Rolf Yeager from Montgomery's team.

To Mostyn, Montgomery said, "We can use all of this stuff." He turned to Yeager. "Get Green, Oliver, and Vickers to help you load this equipment and these supplies into that deuce and a half." He turned back to Mostyn. "It works, right?"

"It did. Not sure if it still does after that storm."

Montgomery nodded. "Check it out, Yeager."

Yeager saluted. "Yes, sir", and left.

Neumeyer said he'd assist the sergeant, and departed.

"Now what about this artifact?" Montgomery asked.

Mostyn motioned for him to follow and walked over to the tent where the golden casket was housed.

"Holy shit, Mostyn!" Montgomery exclaimed, and reached out to touch the shiny metal. "My God, I can see why you've been having problems. This thing is instant wealth."

"That's not all."

"What do you mean?"

"Notice the storm didn't bother this tent?"

"My God, you're right. What's that mean?"

"Nothing good, Gum. Nothing good."

Montgomery didn't reply. He just stared at the golden object and slowly nodded.

From the dunes came the sound of chanting. And Mostyn realized the language the Bedouins were using was R'lyehian.

———

After consulting with Mostyn, Montgomery decided their best chance for defense was the Temple of Tsathoggua. The building was not as sand choked as the Hall of the Great Old Ones, and it had the possibility of entrance and exit through the passageways connecting the main building to the smaller side buildings.

All the while the truck was being loaded with the remaining supplies from Mostyn's team and the spare equipment from the helicopter, the chanting from the dunes droned on.

"What are they up to?" Montgomery asked.

"Nothing good," Mostyn answered. "That language they're chanting in? That's R'lyehian, you know."

"You mean…?"

Mostyn nodded.

"Shit. This isn't good. Hope those backup choppers get here soon. The base has to have heard our mayday by now."

"One would hope."

"What about the coffin?" Montgomery asked.

"Leave it," Mostyn replied.

"Really?"

Mostyn waved his hand to the dunes. "If these guys see us leaving it, maybe they'll leave us alone."

"Good thinking. Okay, we leave it. I think we're ready to go with this load."

"Then let's get a move on. They've left us alone thus far, but let's not press our luck."

Montgomery yelled, "Vickers, Oliver, get that deuce moving. Jacobs, Quarrington, get that machine gun out of the chopper. The rest of you grab the ammo and let's—"

The ground began shaking, knocking people off their feet. Roaring filled the air. A couple of the buildings on the edge of the city collapsed into piles of rubble.

A short distance down the main thoroughfare the ground began pushing up a mound of sand and earth through the stones of the street.

"What the hell do we have to deal with now?" Jones shouted.

"Be glad the earth didn't open up beneath your feet, Jonesy," NicAskill shouted back.

Dotty laughed. "Being swallowed up by a hole in the ground might be our best option."

Mostyn, pointing to the Bedouins on the dunes, yelled back, "They probably have something to do with that." He pointed at the large mound of sand. "So be prepared for anything."

The ground stopped shaking and there in the middle of the main street was a mound of sand some eight to ten feet high and perhaps fifteen feet across. The chanting had stopped and the only sound was that of the wind blowing a fine grit of sand.

"That's it?" Jones said.

As if on cue, the mound began shaking and undulating before breaking open. Out of it poured thousands of ebony, flesh-eating scarab beetles.

22

MUMMIES

"HOLY SHIT!" Jones yelled, and began blasting away at the large bugs.

Mostyn and Montgomery were yelling, "Fall back!", and people were climbing on top of anything and everything.

Lieutenant Jacobs was yelling, "Out of the way! Get out of the way!", and when he had a clear firing path, opened fire with the machine gun in the helicopter.

NicAskill ran to the deuce and a half, stomping on a soft-ball-sized beetle in the process, jumped in the back, rummaged around until she found what she was looking for, took as many as she could carry, jumped back out, and ran back into the chaos.

She saw Doctor Hyde, making her way to the M113, trying to outrun a swarm of beetles. On top of the carrier, Lentz and Munroe were shooting at the bugs and cheering her on.

NicAskill was too far away to help the doctor and watched the speedy beetles close the gap. They were on the doctor's heels when she jumped and tried to grab the metal guard around the lights, missed, and slid down the slanted front of the vehicle, screaming for help.

Within just a second or two Hyde disappeared. She was completely buried in beetles; her screams quickly choked off.

"God," NicAskill said, and swallowed several times to keep her breakfast down. She took a deep breath and focused on the job at hand.

Yelling "Grenade!", NicAskill hurled first one, and then a second thermobaric grenade into the oncoming swarm.

"That's for Doctor Hyde," she shouted.

The blasts produced two great gaping holes in the tsunami of black bugs pouring out of the collapsed mound.

She hurled a third grenade towards the mound. The explosion obliterated thousands more of the bugs, and yet they still kept coming.

Seeing Jones and Neumeyer with jerry cans of fuel, NicAskill hurled two more grenades. The blasts momentarily halted the oncoming waves of beetles, and allowed Jones and Neumeyer time to empty the cans and ignite the fuel to form a barrier that would channel the surging sea of flesh-eating bugs into the path of the helicopter's machine gun. Lieutenant Jacobs opened fire, and the fifty caliber bullets turned the bugs into a gooey mash.

With only two grenades left, NicAskill hurled one for all she was worth toward the remains of the mound. The grenade bounced off some large bugs, landed at the base of the collapsed hill, and exploded. The powerful blast wave completely collapsed what was left of the mound and sealed the opening from which the giant beetles were coming.

Private Vickers threw the deuce and a half into gear and plowed through the last wave of oncoming bugs, drove over the flattened mound, and on into the center of the city.

In the camp, the OUP personnel blasted the remaining bugs with rifle, pistol, and submachine gun fire. A few of the smaller bugs were squashed under booted feet.

When all was quiet, Mostyn looked up at the top of the dunes. The Bedouins were still there. Running through Mostyn's mind was the question, how would uneducated and essentially primitive Bedouins know R'lyehian?

Helene appeared next to him. "What are you looking at, Mostyn Pierce?"

"Those men up there. I don't think they're Arabs."

"I do not think so either."

Mostyn looked at her. "You don't? Why?"

"While you were fighting the insects, I went out there." She pointed to the men out on the salt flat.

"And?"

"I think they are related to my people."

"What makes you think so?"

"Because when I killed one of them, they started shouting in a language that sounded like mine, although I could not understand it."

Mostyn thought a moment. "Could they be descendants of the original inhabitants of Iram and now that the city is no longer buried, they've come back to claim it?"

Helene shrugged. "I do not know, Mostyn Pierce. It would, however, explain why they were chanting in R'lyehian."

"Yes, it would. It would also explain their interest in this place. In a sense they are Keepers. Keepers of the Secrets of Iram."

"Yes, Mostyn Pierce, that is what they are. They are this ancient city's protectors."

"And that means there are going to be more nasty surprises for us before this is over." He looked up at the sky.

The sun was hot and unforgiving. There was not a cloud to be seen. And there were no helicopters, either.

————

The two teams were moving equipment into the temple, when the chanting started up again.

"Now what are they going to throw at us?" Montgomery asked Mostyn.

"Whatever it is, it won't be good." Mostyn went on to explain to Montgomery his idea that these people weren't actually Bedouins, but were, for lack of a better term, the Keepers of the Secrets of Iram.

When Mostyn was finished explaining his theory, Montgomery nodded, and said, "I wish we had more ordinance. Wasn't expecting to fight a small-scale war with demons from the night."

"This is an OUP operation," Mostyn replied. "Or did you forget?"

"Didn't forget. Was just supposed to get you out."

"And you didn't think you might find my people and me in a small-scale war? Have they moved you to a desk job?"

"Very funny, Mostyn. Don't worry, we'll get you out."

"I hope so. Wouldn't want to damage your bragging rights."

"Ha, ha. I have work to do, so I can save your ass. Again. Want to help?"

Mostyn gave Montgomery a slap on the back. "Sure. God helps those who help themselves."

The two leaders set up three defensive positions. The initial line was to hold off the enemy from breaching the temple. The deuce and a half was positioned halfway towards the fountain and rigged with explosives. Rubble was stacked up in front of the main doors to provide cover for the machine guns taken from the helicopter and the armored personnel carrier.

The second line of defense was the raised dais or stage area, inside the temple, where the altar and giant idol were located. The final defense would be made in the chambers below the temple.

To get to the roof of the temple building, one had to use a set of steps on the outside of the building towards the back. Two of Montgomery's people were positioned there: Privates Edward Vickers, and Fifi Oliver. They were equipped with sniper rifles. A three-foot-high wall surrounding the rooftop protected them from anyone shooting at them from down below, but left them open to attack from the men, or Keepers, on the tops of the dunes, who could shoot down on them. For just such a situation they'd been supplied with special OUP protective devices. The downside being that the supernatural protection was of short-term duration.

Montgomery stood in the middle of the temple's main floor, hands on hips, and looked around. "Well, Mostyn, looks good to me. What do you say?"

"I'll tell you what I think in the chopper flying us back to the base."

"Oh, ye of little faith."

"Faith, Gum, has nothing to do with it."

The time was early afternoon, and with everyone in position, Mostyn decided MREs could be handed out. Willie Lee Baker and Doctor Richard Munro walked the positions and handed out the food packets to the men and women. Even more than the food, the bottle of water was especially welcomed. The air was searingly dry.

All the time, the chanting continued uninterrupted. Montgomery had left Mostyn to confer with Lieutenant Clifton, and Mostyn had sought out Jones, NicAskill, and Neumeyer.

"They're cooking up something," Jones said. "The question is, what?"

"We're sitting ducks here," NicAskill added.

"I'd say more like fish in a barrel," Neumeyer countered. "Provided they get through our initial line of defense."

"Or whatever it is they decide to throw at us, instead of coming themselves," NicAskill said. "It's just a matter of time. And time is on their side."

"Hopefully we'll hold them off long enough for the cavalry to get here," Jones said.

"That's basically where we are at," Mostyn said, confirming Jones's comment.

"Here they come!" Montgomery yelled.

Mostyn ran out to the portico. He looked across the central area, where the fountain was, towards the Hall of the Great Old Ones. Pouring out of the doors were a whole hell of a lot of mummies.

23

ATTACK

VICKERS AND OLIVER activated the Class I demidaemonus to shield them from the shooters on the dunes above, and opened fire. Their job was to methodically take out the Keepers on the other side of the valley. Every time they squeezed the triggers and their rifles fired, there were two less men chanting.

Lieutenants Jacobs and Quarrington, the chopper's pilot and co-pilot, crewed the machine gun taken from the chopper, while Private Ambrose Greene manned the machine gun Mostyn had taken from the armored personnel carrier. Both guns opened fire on the initial wave of mummies that surged past the deuce and a half.

Mostyn, standing next to Montgomery in front of the doors to the temple, watched the brown, cloth-wrapped undead corpses approach. They moved much like the zombies he'd seen in those old zombie films of his youth, only faster. Since joining the OUP, Mostyn no longer watched zombie films. Or any horror films, for that matter.

He leaned over to Montgomery and said, "Now?"

Montgomery nodded and pressed the button on the detonator. The deuce and a half exploded into a towering inferno of flames. Great numbers of mummies were instantly incinerated, and the flames effectively blocked the path of the undead onslaught. The two machine guns sent streams of lead into the ancient undead, the desiccated bodies exploding into clouds of dry ancient dust.

"The resin on those wrappings is very flammable," Mostyn observed.

"We can use that to our advantage," Montgomery replied.

Mostyn nodded and went inside the temple. He found Jones, and told him to find everything combustible that he could. They'd torch those things in hand to hand combat if they had to.

"I'm on it, Boss," Jones said, with a big smile on his face.

Mostyn rejoined Montgomery, and watched the machine guns mow down the last of the mummies on the temple side of the burning truck.

"This will give us a breather until the truck burns out," Montgomery said.

"How are we doing on ammunition?" Mostyn asked.

"We're running low on the machine guns."

"I have Jones working on some flammables."

"Good. We'll probably need them sooner rather than later."

The battlefield was quiet except for the firing of the sniper rifles on the roof and the rifle shots from the Keepers attempting to take out the snipers.

Mostyn and Montgomery watched the flames gradually die down.

"Get ready, people," Montgomery called out.

A mummy trying to thread its way through the dying

flames stumbled, fell, and caught fire. Another one, following it, made it around the truck. Then there was a second, and a third.

Corporal Piper Timms aimed her rifle, squeezed the trigger, and watched the first mummy's chest explode in a shower of dust and bone fragments. Head, arms, legs, and the remainder of the torso collapsed in a heap. Sergeant Yeager joined in, and a second mummy blew apart.

In short order, however, the flow of the undead pouring around the truck was too great to be stopped by Timms and Yeager alone. The machine guns opened fire.

Mummies blew apart in a continual shower of dust and bone fragments, yet the mindless horde continued to advance.

Jones showed up with eight makeshift torches and matches. "I don't know how long these things will last," he said. "Probably best to torch one of those things and then shove it back into the others so they catch on fire."

"Good idea, Jones," Mostyn said.

"I also have a surprise set up should they or anyone else get through the doors here."

"Thanks," Mostyn replied.

Jones went back inside and Mostyn distributed torches and matches to everyone holding the line at the front door.

A bullet hit one of the stone steps, ricocheted, and caught Lieutenant Jacobs in the chest. He fell back onto the stone floor of the portico. Lieutenant Quarrington and Captain Montgomery began administering emergency first aid to stop the bleeding and keep him alive.

Mostyn took over the machine gun and continued firing until the box of belted ammunition was empty. He looked around the gun. There was no more ammo, and the mummies were now surging up the steps towards the portico.

"Light the torches!" Mostyn yelled. He grabbed a torch, struck a match, and ignited the incendiary weapon.

A mummy loomed up before Mostyn, who jammed the flaming torch into the stomach of the undead thing. The resin-soaked cloths caught fire. Mostyn shoved and pushed the burning thing into the other mummies coming up the steps behind it.

The tinder-dry things burst into flames in a cascading domino effect, eliminating scores of the enemy.

Sergeant Rolf Yeager swung his torch like a baseball bat, sending the head of one of the undead in a line drive towards the fountain. The headless body shambled closer, arms outstretched, hands grasping for Yeager's throat. Yeager swung the torch back and connected with the mummy's torso. It toppled over to the side in a mass of flames, igniting several other mummies.

Another mummy surged forward, swinging the thigh bone of one of its fellow undead. The makeshift club caught Yeager on the shoulder and down he went, losing hold of his torch in the process. Several mummies piled on top of him.

Mostyn, swinging his torch back and forth, was holding half a dozen of the undead at bay. He took out his pistol with his other hand and opened fire. Recalling that the Egyptians would leave the heart in the body before embalming because they believed it contained the soul, Mostyn shot the mummies in the left side of their chests and watched them crumble instantly into a fine powder.

Montgomery was yelling, "Fall back!", and desperately trying to get his people inside the temple.

Jones appeared in the doorway, shotgun in hand. Greene, Timms, Quarrington, Clifton, Mostyn, and Montgomery ran through the open doorway. Not surviving his wound, Jacobs's body was left behind. Jones, like a modern-day King Kull, or Conan, blasted away with the shotgun, blowing apart the things and keeping the horde at bay, while the others began closing the massive doors.

With just enough room for Jones to slip through, he fired a parting shot, slipped through the opening, and the doors slammed shut. Rubble was pushed in front of them to help keep them closed.

Montgomery looked over his people. "Where are Oliver and Vickers?"

Jones shook his head. "Not here."

A look of disgust crossed Montgomery's face. "That damn demidaemonus must've crapped out on them." He shook his head. "They were good people. Jacobs and Yeager, too."

"We need to get in position, Gum," Mostyn said.

"You're right. The next wave will probably be those damn camel jockeys."

Everyone fell back to the raised stage area, where the altar was located and the statue of Tsathoggua lurked in the darkness.

Along the front of the stage was an assemblage of chairs, couches, tables, shelving, beds, and what have you, creating a makeshift barrier which provided the teams some manner of protection and cover.

Dotty sought out Mostyn, and found him looking over the entrance to one of the side buildings. She stood next to him and put her arm around his waist.

"The sand has left us just enough room to make it through this doorway, should we need to use it," she said.

"Mother Nature leaving us a way out. Hopefully."

Dotty snorted. She turned towards Mostyn and he turned to face her.

"The shit could hit the fan anytime now, Mostyn."

"Thanks for letting me know, Kemper."

She rolled her eyes. "Look. Don't make this difficult."

"Sorry."

"Pierce, I want you to know that in spite of our weird situation — you know, with Helene."

Mostyn nodded.

"I love you, and I don't want to be with anyone else."

"I know, Dot, and I'm sorry. Believe me—"

Dotty put her right index finger on his mouth. "I know. I just wanted to tell you. This might be the end of the line for one or both of us, and I wanted you to know."

Mostyn held her face in his hands and kissed her. "I love you, Dotty Kemper. And we are going to get out of this."

She pulled his hands away. "You don't know that. I hope you're right, but we don't know that we're going to make it."

Mostyn looked into her eyes. "You're right. No, we don't," he admitted. Yet the tone of his voice said otherwise.

"At least we had a chance at love, and I'm thankful for that."

"Me, too, Dot. Me, too."

Montgomery's voice bellowed, "They're coming! Prepare for attack!"

Mostyn turned and looked across the temple. Standing in each of the windows on the other side of the building was one of the Keepers. The Keepers of the Secrets of Iram.

He looked up at the windows on his side of the building. From each window a rope reached to the floor, and men were either abseiling down them or using the rope to help them descend the mounds of sand that had come in the windows.

Dotty fired her pistol and the one just off to their left fell to the floor just feet from where Dotty and Mostyn were standing. He was still alive. He spoke in a language unknown to them, hatred apparent on his face. Then Dotty plunged her knife into his throat.

The OUP personnel opened fire and the Keepers began dropping like flies hit with pesticide spray. But for every one that took a bullet, two more took his place.

A boom sounded throughout the temple and the doors shook.

"Nuts," Mostyn said. "They're using a battering ram to take down the doors."

"Yeah, then there will be more of these goddamn Keepers than we can count."

"Come on, Dot, let's go." He grabbed her hand, and they ran back to the barricaded stage area, bullets thudding into the sand around them.

They clambered up the steps, and dove behind the barricade. Bullets thudded into pieces of furniture and ricocheted off stone.

The OUP riflemen kept picking off the Keepers coming in from the windows, but at least a dozen had made it to the floor of the temple and were shooting back. The booms of the battering ram were a steady tattoo.

Only a matter of time, Mostyn thought, pulling the trigger on his pistol and sending a Keeper to whatever hell they inhabited.

There was a boom accompanied by the sound of wood splintering.

"Jones!" Mostyn yelled, "Ready your surprise!"

"All set, Boss!" Jones yelled back.

Mostyn watched a Keeper vanish, only to see a moment later just his legs sticking above the temple floor. *Go, Helene*, he thought.

The battering ram hit the doors, there was the sound of wood tearing, and the massive things fell to the temple floor.

Scurrying over the broken doors and the makeshift barricade that had helped to hold them closed came a tsunami of men screaming in an unknown language.

24

RECON

THE KEEPERS of the Secrets of Iram swept into the temple, screaming what Mostyn assumed were battle cries, and firing their weapons. Up and down the line, the OUP personnel returned fire.

Bullets thunked into the barricade and ricocheted off the stone steps leading up to the stage area.

Mostyn took his time, making sure his aim was true. He slowly squeezed the trigger, and the rifle fired. One of the men charging towards his position flew backwards as if someone had yanked a rope tied around his waist.

Scores of men were running up the central aisle of the temple. Jones yelled, "Cover!", and pressed a button on the small box he held in his hand. Explosions ripped through the center of the temple, tossing men like rag dolls, and igniting the gasoline and diesel fuel Jones had hidden in the sand.

Mostyn looked out over the battlefield. There were so many bodies lying in the bloodied sand he couldn't count them. The smell of burning flesh was strong. The only sound was the moans of the dying. Even the Keepers in the windows had disappeared.

They'll be back, Mostyn thought. *They just need time to regroup.*

And in a matter of just a few minutes, Keepers reappeared in the windows and the battle resumed.

When the flames from Jones's surprise had burned themselves out, the Keepers in the windows started whistling, and moments later a screaming horde poured through the shattered doorway at the front of the temple. At the same time, from the doorway to the side building where Mostyn and Dotty had chatted, Privates Fifi Oliver and Edward Vickers charged, their rifles blazing.

Mostyn saw a big smile appear on Montgomery's face.

As the two neared the stage area of the temple, they hurled grenades into the throng of the attacking Keepers, ran up the steps, and jumped over the barricade. The explosions killed dozens of the enemy. Oliver and Vickers took up positions on the firing line and began firing their rifles, sending a stream of bullets into the tsunami of human attackers.

Jones and NicAskill, both yelling, "Cover!", hurled thermobaric grenades into the surging melee. The grenades exploded in two sheets of flame, sucking up the oxygen in the vicinity of the blasts, and hammering everything in the path of the powerful shockwave. Even the OUP teams felt the pressure of the blast.

Mostyn peered over the barricade. He guessed there had to be at least a couple hundred dead, or on their way to a hellish beyond. The blasts had cleared the enemy from the temple floor and from the windows. There were no living Keepers to be seen.

Montgomery, in a crouch, ran over to Mostyn. "How soon do you think they'll be back?"

"I don't know. But I don't think they'll take long. They know we're trapped."

"That's what I was thinking. We've held them off thus far. Maybe they'll just wait."

"I don't think so. And whatever they throw at us next, won't be pleasant."

"What more can they throw at us?"

"Hell itself. This is an OUP operation, remember?"

"So you keep reminding me."

"My team had better be armed to the teeth on the next mission, or I'll refuse to go. We've pretty much been caught with our pants down on this one."

"It was supposed to be a fairly quiet archaeological recon, wasn't it?"

"It was."

"If it's any consolation, I'm with you. Prepare for the worst. Shall we see what these jokers are up to?"

"Sure. Good idea." Mostyn and Montgomery both stood and Mostyn addressed the teams. "Hold the line. The captain and I are going to take a look-see and find out what the enemy is up to."

"I will go with you, Mostyn Pierce," Helene said. She walked up to the two men, linked her arms with theirs and the three dematerialized.

Mostyn heard Fifi Oliver say, "Holy shit! Did you see that?"

Montgomery's thoughts came to Mostyn, *What the hell is going on?*

Helene replied and let Mostyn also receive the message, *Just relax, Captain Montgomery. You are in a dematerialized state. You are invisible.*

Well, I'll be damned, Montgomery thought. *So you're the one the rumors are about. Mostyn, you lucky—*

Careful, Gum, she can read your thoughts.

Oh, geez, ma'am, I'm sorry.

Helene's giggle sounded in both men's minds.

They moved across the carnage of bodies that covered the length of the temple floor.

This is so weird, Montgomery thought.

Once outside the building, they saw that the Keepers had surrounded the temple complex, and were once again chanting in a low, droning monotone.

Mostyn surveyed them. It was clear to him that they were gearing up for some new attack. And that they themselves most likely wouldn't be making the assault. Something else would take their place.

Sorry Mostyn Pierce, Helene thought.

Mostyn and Montgomery suddenly found themselves visible.

"What the hell just happened?" Montgomery said.

"I don't know. This is not the norm."

"Talk about feeling naked."

A shot rang out, glanced off a pillar, sending a stone chip whizzing past Mostyn's ear.

The two men hunkered down behind a pillar, and then disappeared.

I am sorry, Mostyn Pierce and Captain Montgomery. Doctor Bardon sent a message and I could not keep us all dematerialized.

Bardon got a message to you? Montgomery thought. *From Washington?*

Yes, Helene replied.

What did he say? Mostyn thought.

He is coming. He sends his apologies. He did not realize how dangerous this mission would become.

Wait a minute, Montgomery thought. *How can Bardon talk to you?*

It is his way, Helene replied.

What the hell does that mean? Montgomery asked.

Mostyn laughed. *Don't even bother, Gum.*

The three returned to the OUP defensive position, where they rematerialized.

"Listen up, people," Mostyn said. "Bardon is coming. The danger here caught even him unawares. Until he gets here, however, we are on our own. As you can hear, the chanting has resumed. So it's obvious the Keepers of this place have cooked up something else for us. Jones, select whoever you need, and barricade the doorway the best you can. The cavalry is coming. We just don't know when."

"On it," Jones replied.

"Whoever isn't with Jones, keep your eyes trained on those windows and shoot whatever comes through them."

Jones, NicAskill, Neumeyer, Quarrington, and Greene went to the front of the building to do what they could to block the entrance. The remaining men and women kept watch on the windows. Mostyn and Montgomery kept an eye on the side entrances to the other buildings connected to the temple.

Time passed slowly, and even in the dim interior of the temple the heat was oppressive.

Mostyn looked at the doorway that led to the smaller building next to the temple and wondered if it wouldn't be better to take up a defensive position there.

His thoughts were interrupted by Jones yelling, "They're

coming! Those goddamn mummies are coming — and this time they're armed with spears!"

Jones and his workgroup ran back to the defensive barricade.

"They look like they're right out of one of those movies," he said. "You know, the Greeks or Romans. Marching in rows with spears."

"A phalanx," Mostyn said.

Montgomery shook his head. "A what?"

"Ancient Greek battle formation," Mostyn explained. "Rank upon rank of armored men with shields and long spears. The most formidable fighting formation of the ancient world. Alexander the Great conquered the known world with it."

"Yeah, but we have guns," Montgomery said.

"Gum, how much ammunition do we have left?" Mostyn asked.

Montgomery said nothing. It was Jones who gave Mostyn his answer. "Can you spell shish kabob?"

25

TSATHOGGUA VENIT VIVIT

JONES'S BARRICADE slowed the advance of the mummies. However, the OUP teams couldn't take full advantage of the situation because the Keepers had once again positioned riflemen in the windows to pin down Mostyn's and Montgomery's people.

Lieutenant Texas Quarrington and Private Fifi Oliver used the sniper rifles to take out the shooters. But for every man they shot, another took his place.

Lieutenant Scarlet Clifton, Corporal Piper Timms, Private Ambrose Greene, and Special Forces Agent Hal Neumeyer picked off the mummies clambering over the barricade.

"Shoot for their hearts," Mostyn instructed. "That's the only way to stop the mummies using just one bullet."

Mostyn watched as Timms readjusted her aim and squeezed the trigger. Down range, a mummy coming over the barricade collapsed into a pile of dust.

"Good shot," Mostyn said, as Timms's head exploded in a shower of bone, blood, and brains.

Making a statement regarding the sexual relationship between the Keepers and their mothers, Mostyn picked up Timms's rifle and proceeded to dispatch Keeper after Keeper to whatever hell had spawned them until he ran out of ammunition. He reloaded and continued shooting.

The mummies were coming in faster than they could be destroyed and had succeeded in forming a unit of fifteen across and six rows deep, that was marching up the center aisle over the bodies of the dead Keepers.

NicAskill hurled her last thermobaric grenade. The blast incinerated the phalanx of mummies and blew Keepers out of the windows.

"Maybe we'll get a bit of a reprieve now," Montgomery said, as he came over to confer with Mostyn.

"Until they regroup," Mostyn said. He turned to Jones. "Do you have your phone?"

"Always, Boss."

"See if you can get Bardon."

"Will do."

To Montgomery, he said, "What's our ammunition like?"

"We're down to our last magazines. The cavalry needs to get here very soon."

"We're going to have to save the ammo, I think, Gum, and fight the next attack hand to hand."

Montgomery nodded. "It's looking like it."

"And I think we need to barricade ourselves in the small building there." Mostyn pointed.

"Good idea. Those shooters up in the windows are murder."

"Boss, I got Colonel Pettibone on the sat phone," Jones said, running over to Mostyn.

"Glad to see they got the satellite back in position," Mostyn said. He took the phone from Jones.

"Mostyn here, Pettibone."

"We're at an ETA of five minutes, Mostyn. What's your situation?"

"Unknown number of hostiles who have the ability to bring the dead back to life. Unknown number of said dead attacking us. The dead are mummies."

"Say again, Mostyn."

"We're being attacked by mummies. They're flammable, though, so that is an advantage to us."

"Gotcha. Can you get to an open space or a roof top?"

"Negative on the open space. Will try for a rooftop. Look for the central square of the city. We'll be on the roof of the temple to the south of the central square. To the south of the thing that looks like a giant fountain."

"Roger that, Mostyn. Get to that rooftop for extraction."

"On our way, Pettibone."

Mostyn ended the call, and handed the phone back to Jones.

"Listen up, people," Mostyn said. "The cavalry is on its way. There's to be a rooftop extraction."

"The stairs to the roof are out that door, Mr. Mostyn," Fifi Oliver said, and pointed to the door she meant.

"Thank you—" Mostyn, however, didn't get to finish what he was going to say, for over Jones's barricade came scores of spear-wielding mummies.

"Aw, shit," Jones said. "This is getting old awfully fast."

"Get ready for hand-to-hand combat," Montgomery called out. "Save your ammo. Ready bayonets if you have them."

Mostyn added, "Remember to get the heart. Anything else, and they keep on coming."

The mummies shambled across the temple floor and began mounting the steps to the stage area, jabbing with their spears across the barricade.

Jones twisted to miss a spear thrust, grabbed the spear, wrenched it from the mummy's grasp, and drove the backend of the spear into the thing's chest. It disintegrated before his eyes.

The undead began climbing over the barricade. NicAskill rolled, got under the spear point of one of the things, and stabbed the mummy in the heart with her combat knife. It disintegrated. She grabbed its spear and attacked the undead with gusto as they came over the barrier.

Helene dematerialized a mummy about to spear Lieutenant Scarlett Clifton, who was fighting another mummy, and rematerialized it in the floor of the temple.

Mostyn parried a spear thrust with the rifle he'd picked up, and then jammed the bayonet into the mummy's heart.

Dotty Kemper, Waldemar Lentz, Richard Munroe, and Willie Lee Baker were behind the front line waiting for a chance to make a run for the exit and the stairs to the rooftop. They were armed with submachine guns.

Mostyn fought his way to Jones and retrieved the OUP sat phone.

Montgomery was yelling, "Shift to the left!"

Mostyn waved to Dotty, indicating her group should make a run for it.

The rest of the OUP personnel shifted in an attempt to provide cover for the specialist personnel to make their escape.

Dotty and the other specialists were almost to the door leading to the smaller temple and outside when the ground shook, knocking everyone off their feet, humans and mummies alike.

A cracking sound reverberated throughout the temple.

Mostyn got to his knees, pressed the button to answer the call from Pettibone, and saw what was making the cracking sound.

The statue of Tsathoggua was beginning to move.

26

AND THEN IT WAS GONE

"Mostyn, are you there? Mostyn?"

Mostyn watched chunks of stone fall away from the giant statue and saw the eyelid blink.

"Pettibone, you better get here quick. Because this statue of Tsathoggua is coming alive."

"We're here. We're taking gunfire. We'll clear off the tops of the dunes. Get your people to the roof."

"On our way, Pettibone."

Mostyn hooked the phone on his belt, leaving the channel open. "Everybody up. Let's go. Oliver, lead the way to the roof."

"Yes, sir. Follow me."

The mummies weren't moving, but the statue of the hideous Great Old One continued to make loud cracking sounds and Mostyn watched chunks of stone fall away, revealing what looked like a slimy, mucilaginous skin underneath. It was like watching a chick coming out of its shell.

Following Oliver were the OUP civilians, including Helene.

Montgomery called out, "Your personnel next, Mostyn. And that includes you."

Mostyn yelled, "Jones, NicAskill, Neumeyer. Go!" To Montgomery he said, "The captain leaves the ship last."

Before Montgomery could respond, several mummies got up and one speared Montgomery's leg. Mostyn fired a bullet from his pistol, and the mummy disintegrated.

Clifton, Quarrington, and Greene, formed a line between the mummies and Mostyn, who helped Montgomery to the exit.

Mostyn grabbed the sat phone off his belt. To Greene, he said, "Get Gum out of here." Into the phone, he yelled, "What's your status, Pettibone?"

"We've cleared the dunes overlooking the rooftop. Get your people up here."

"They're on their way."

"What about you?"

Mostyn pulled the trigger on his pistol and a mummy collapsed into a pile of dust and bones, its spear thudding into the sand.

"Thanks, Mostyn," Scarlett Clifton said.

Pointing to the exit, Mostyn yelled, "You and Quarrington get the hell out of here!" Into the phone, he said, "Pettibone, you need to blast the inside of this hall. That statue is just about fully alive."

"Roger, Mostyn. Get yourself out."

"On my way."

Mostyn went through the doorway, turning two of his undead pursuers to dust and bones. He ran down the corridor. To his left was an open doorway. Helene materialized.

"This way, my husband."

"You shouldn't be here."

"Someone needed to guide you. I was the logical choice."

Shambling down the corridor were a trio of spear-wielding mummies. One by one they disappeared.

"Man, I wish we could bottle that."

Helene smiled. "Come, Mostyn Pierce."

Mostyn took her hand, she kissed him, and they dematerialized.

Two clouds of atoms glided swiftly through the open doorway towards the stair steps to the roof. There was a deafening roar, the ground shook, and sheets of flame shot out of the windows of the temple. Cracks appeared in the temple wall.

The temple isn't going to last much longer, Mostyn thought. *We must hurry.*

Up the stairs their atoms flew and out onto the roof. A helicopter was waiting for them, along with Jones, carrying a submachine gun.

The two re-materialized.

"Good to see you, Boss," Jones said.

"Why aren't you in the chopper?" Mostyn asked.

"Just making sure it was you and not some uglies."

"Thanks."

"Go on. I got your back."

Mostyn and Helene got into the helicopter, followed by Jones, and the chopper lifted off. They put on headsets so they could hear each other and the crew of the helicopter.

Looking out the open door, where the machine gunner was in position behind the gun, waiting for action, Mostyn noticed a ring of Keepers around the fountain. They were on their knees, alternately bowing and sitting up, their arms raised above their heads.

"Is it my eyes, or is that thing glowing?" Mostyn asked.

"It is glowing, Mostyn Pierce."

"They're trying to open the gate. Jones, are those charges in place?"

"They were. Wasn't able to check after the storm."

"I think it is too late, Mostyn Pierce."

Mostyn followed Helene's pointing finger. High in the sky above the fountain, clouds had formed, a churning and roiling coruscation of an inky blackness that was not of this earth.

"Jones, you'd better set off that detonator."

A brilliant beam of white light shot from the central obelisk of the fountain, a laser beam cutting open a door into another dimension.

A line appeared, and then tentacles pushed their way through the slender opening, forcing the cut in the fabric between dimensions to open wider, to become a gaping hole, a doorway from one dimension, a dimension of horrors, into our own.

"Jones," Mostyn said. "Detonator."

"It's not working, Boss. That storm must've messed something up."

"Wait, Mostyn Pierce. Look! It's Doctor Bardon."

Mostyn followed Helene's pointing finger. There, in a column of swirling sand a short distance away, an effigy was forming. Clearly visible was the bespectacled face of Doctor Rafe Bardon.

The three watched as, within seconds, the rotund body of the OUP director took form out of the swirling chaos. The effigy brought its hands together as though it was strangling someone or something. At the same time, the Keepers surrounding the fountain clutched at their throats.

The white light shooting into the heavens flickered, as did the glow emanating from the obelisk of the fountain itself.

In a matter of moments, Mostyn watched as the Keepers collapsed, kicked their legs a last time, and went still. The light vanished from the fountain and the tear in the wall between dimensions closed. The clouds dissipated, and so did the sand effigy of Doctor Bardon.

"Holy shit!" Jones said. "That was incredible!"

Mostyn nodded. "Learn something new about Doctor Bardon every mission," he said, and heard a new voice over his headset.

"Lieutenant Sanders here, Mr. Mostyn. We have orders to retrieve the coffin you discovered."

Mostyn shook his head. "I think we'd best leave it."

"The orders are from Doctor Bardon, himself."

Mostyn sighed. "Okay. It's at the camp."

"Can you point out which tent?"

"Sure. Probably the only one still standing and in perfect condition."

When the helicopter was over the camp, Mostyn pointed out the tent, and Sanders landed the helicopter in an open space some distance away.

The machine gun was swung out of the way, a ramp extended, and Mostyn and Jones followed two crewmen and a flat, rectangular robot that used tracks instead of wheels out of the chopper. "Better in the sand," one of the crewmen informed Mostyn.

The four men and the robot travelled to the tent, and once inside, one of the crewmen pressed a button. The very top of the robot rose so that it was level with the bottom of the gold casket. The men then slid the casket onto the robot's platform, which was lowered so it was once again atop the body of the machine. The men strapped the casket down so it couldn't move.

The men, robot, and casket returned to the helicopter. The robot rolled up the ramp and was secured by the crewmen to prevent it from moving. Mostyn and Jones returned to their seats.

When everyone was belted in, the chopper powered up, and took off, circling the camp before it began its journey north.

Looking out the open door, past the machine gunner, Mostyn saw, over the western edge of the city, black clouds forming. He spoke into the mouthpiece of his headset. "Sanders, we have to dump that coffin. We're about to have company."

"What do you mean?"

"Look at the western edge of the ruins."

In his ear, Mostyn heard, "What the hell?"

From the swirling pitch-black mass of clouds, a funnel had descended and a swirling pillar of sand had risen to meet it.

"Hell is right, Sanders. Dump the coffin."

"But we have Bardon's orders."

"You see that face that just formed in the clouds? That is the face on this coffin we have, and if it catches us, you can kiss your ass goodbye."

Sanders brought the helicopter about and saw that he was flying straight into a giant face with a massively wide-open mouth that revealed a blackness darker than eternal night.

The chopper made a hard turn to port. Mostyn began yelling at the crewmen to unstrap the robot and send it out of the chopper.

"We can't," he heard, "the machine gun is in the way."

"Then unstrap the coffin and we'll push it out," Mostyn replied.

"But our orders…"

"To hell with your orders. I'm in charge of this mission. Cut the goddamn coffin loose!"

The crewmen began unstrapping the coffin. Mostyn looked out the open door behind the chopper. The cloud face was gaining on them, looming ever larger, it's massive open mouth blacker than a black hole.

The last strap was loosed, and Jones and Mostyn joined the crewmen as all four pushed the gold casket out the open door.

Sanders made another sharp turn to port, sent the chopper into a steep climb to gain more altitude, and then leveled off. He turned the helicopter so that the open bay was facing the ruins.

They watched the casket get caught in a powerful updraft and saw it get sucked into the open mouth of the cloud man.

The midnight clouds and swirling sand engulfed the city of Iram. Iram of the Thousand Pillars. Iram of the Old Ones.

There was a massive rotating black storm that swallowed up the entire valley in which Iram had been built. Strong winds buffeted the helicopter. And in a flash the clouds vanished and the wind was gone. Looking out the open bay of the chopper, all Mostyn saw was sand stretching off to the horizon.

EPILOGUE

DOCTOR RAFE BARDON lit his pipe. A cloud of sweet-smelling Virginia pipe tobacco ascended to the ceiling. He was sitting behind his heavy black walnut desk. Across from him sat Special Agent in Charge Pierce Mostyn.

"Mr. Baker got some magnificent photographs, Pierce, my boy. Magnificent photographs."

"He always does, sir."

"Very true, very true." There was a pause, while Bardon puffed on his pipe and looked over at the statues of Cthulhu and Shub-Niggurath that adorned either end of his sideboard. Trophies from a previous mission.

His eyes slid over to look at the corner of the room by Cthulhu. Not too long ago that corner seemed to be disintegrating, or perhaps it was opening into another dimension.

In either case, Bardon thought, *the talisman seems to be holding. And a good thing too.*

He looked back at Mostyn. "This was a costly mission, Pierce, and I am afraid it is all my fault. I was entirely too cavalier in thinking that there wouldn't be, ah, protective measures in place."

"All missions are dangerous, sir. We learn from our mistakes."

Bardon puffed on his pipe and smiled. "At least we're supposed to. I promise you, Pierce, I will make sure you have adequate support next time."

"Thank you, sir." Mostyn let a moment pass before he continued. "That was a rather spectacular display you put on, sir."

Bardon chuckled. "It got the job done."

"How did you do it, sir?"

Bardon set his pipe in the ashtray. The joviality left his face. "Everything has its price, Pierce. Everything. Sometimes the price is high. So high you don't want to pay it — and yet you must. There is no alternative. Let us simply say I do not wish to pay that price again anytime soon."

Mostyn let it go. He knew Bardon had told him all he was going to say on the matter.

The director got up and walked over to the sideboard. He poured himself a glass of port, and held the decanter up to Mostyn, who nodded.

Mostyn didn't care much for port, but when Bardon offered, one didn't refuse. The director didn't offer his port to just anybody.

Mostyn stood and took the glass from his boss. Both men returned to their seats.

"How is Special Agent NicAskill working out?"

Mostyn sipped the sweet, somewhat fruity and spicy wine. "Fine, sir. She's a very capable agent."

"So her relationship with Mr. Jones isn't a problem?"

Mostyn almost choked on his wine. "What?" he gasped.

"Oh, dear me, you don't know. I'm sorry. I thought their relationship was obvious."

"It's news to me, sir. So I guess I can say, no, it isn't a problem."

"That's good."

Mostyn finished his port. "It's a shame Iram is once again buried beneath the sand. At the same time, it's a relief."

"After what you've been through, I'm sure it is."

Mostyn thought it odd that Bardon didn't express sorrow over the loss of the city. Then again this was Doctor Bardon he was talking to.

"You have a couple weeks off, Pierce, my boy. Enjoy them."

"I will, sir."

Mostyn stood and Bardon did also. They shook hands.

"And give Doctor Kemper and Miss Dubreuil my regards."

"I will do that, sir."

Mostyn left, and Bardon resumed his seat. He brought up a window on his computer, and in a moment was talking with the US ambassador to Saudi Arabia.

"How are the negotiations proceeding, Mr. Wadsworth?"

"I think they are going well, Director Bardon. We should have everything wrapped up here within the next week."

"And the Saudis suspect nothing as to the true nature of our mission?"

"They suspect nothing."

"Good. Thank you, Mr. Wadsworth. Let me know when everything is concluded."

"I will, Mr. Director."

The computer window went blank and Bardon picked up his pipe, relit it, and leaned back in his chair. He'd have to make sure to renew the spell which was making the Saudis amenable to cooperating and kept them ignorant of the real nature of the US mission.

Bardon brought up a map of the Rub al-Khali. At a certain latitude and longitude there was an X on the map.

Everything did indeed have its price, Bardon thought. *And though costly, some things were very much worth the price.*

———

As Mostyn opened the door to get into his car, he paused, and looked at the nondescript building that housed the Office of Unidentified Phenomena headquarters.

He thought of Bardon, and he thought of the recent mission. Iram of the Pillars, or the Old Ones. That city, which for untold eons had lain hidden beneath the sand, whose guardians had, after the city had become exposed, almost succeeded in unleashing an unimaginable horror on the earth, and now was once again buried beneath the sand.

He thought of those monstrous gelatinous forms of physical insanity from another dimension. That they had actually walked upon and ruled the earth, albeit eons before humans came into existence. And in the great cycle of things would undoubtedly do so again.

And what of us? Mostyn thought. *What of us, who have looked into the abyss of eternal night and know that whatever we do, it is all pointless?*

A WORD FROM CW

I hope you enjoyed *Demon in the Dunes*.

If you did, please leave a review where you bought the book and on your favorite social media sites. Your review is like word of mouth advertising. And it is pure gold.

Enter my World

Enter my world. A world of terror on a cosmic scale. Just click, tap, or scan the QR code below.

Fear is the most primal of human emotions. And fear of the unknown is the most terrifying of all fears.

If you are new to the Pierce Mostyn Paranormal Investigations series, then *Demons in the Dunes* is an excellent entry point into the series and into my world.

In addition to my Pierce Mostyn Paranormal Investigations books, I've written short stories set in the world of the macabre and arcane. Many of which are only available to folks on my mailing list.

So just click, tap, or scan the QR code to enter my world of terror and the macabre. You will get a free copy of *The Feeder* and you'll get my monthly email of news and curated contact. Terror awaits!

CONTINUE THE ADVENTURE!

The paranormal investigations of Pierce Mostyn continue in *Van Dyne's Zuvembies*. When Hate Makes Life Worth Living!

Valdis Damien van Dyne is back! And once again, the diabolical mastermind is preparing to launch a wave of terror as a prelude to taking over the world.

What starts out as a series of similar, but unrelated murders, soon begins to take on the signature of van Dyne's handiwork. But what has he unleashed on the world this time? Special Agent in Charge Pierce Mostyn and his team race against the clock to find where the infamous Black Brew is being made to stop van Dyne from infecting New York and other large metro areas. But will Mostyn do so in time to save the world from nightmarish terror?

Van Dyne's Zuvembies is the seventh book in CW Hawes's Pierce Mostyn Paranormal Investigations series.

If you love weird fiction, horror, monsters, humor, thrilling action, and the Cthulhu Mythos, get in on Pierce Mostyn's adventure today — if you dare!

Van Dyne's Zuvembies is available at your favorite online store. Check it out!

BOOKS BY CW HAWES

CW is a multi-genre author.

The books below are portals to his many exciting worlds. And no AI was used in the writing of these books. Books by a human for a human.

Pierce Mostyn Paranormal Investigations

The X-Files meets Cthulhu. Pierce Mostyn does battle with inter-dimensional monsters bent on the destruction of humanity.

Nightmare in Agate Bay
Stairway to Hell
Terror in the Shadows
Van Dyne's Vampires
The Medusa Ritual
Demons in the Dunes
Van Dyne's Zuvembies
In the Shadow of the Mountains of Madness

Justinia Wright Private Investigator Mysteries

Justinia Wright is the PI with panache. These slow burn mysteries, written in homage to Rex Stout's Nero Wolfe, are sure to satisfy your craving for intriguing puzzles, quirky characters, and wise-cracking humor.

Vampire House and Other Early Cases of Justinia Wright, PI
Festival of Death
Trio in Death-Sharp Minor
But Jesus Never Wept
The Conspiracy Game
A Nest of Spies
When Friends Must Die
Death Makes a House Call
To Right a Wrong
The Nine Deadly Dolls
Ripples on the Pond
Christmas with the Wrights
Minneapolis's Finest
Jack in the Box
Sauerkraut Days
Justinia Wright Private Investigator Omnibus Edition

Magnolia Bluff Crime Chronicles

Tense slow burn mysteries set in our favorite town in the Texas Hill Country.

Death Wears a Crimson Hat
Ten Million Ways to Die
Who Mourns Elektra?
Death by Moonlight

The Rocheport Saga

A post-apocalyptic adventure series in the style of cozy catastrophes such as *Earth Abides* and *Day of the Triffids*. Join Bill Arthur as he strives to build a new and better world on the ashes of the old.

The Morning Star
The Shining City
The Divided City
The Troubled City
By Leaps and Bounds
Freedom's Freehold
Take to the Sky

Decopunk

Alternative history adventures in a world where World War II never happened and swing is still king.

From the Files of Lady Dru Drummond
The Moscow Affair
The Golden Fleece Affair

Rand Hart Adventures
Rand Hart and the Pajama Putsch

Tales of the Macabre

For the horror lover in you.
Do One Thing For Me
Metamorphosis
What the Next Day Brings

Ancient History

Anthologies

Enjoy CW's stories in these short story collections.

The Phantom Games

Beyond the Sea

Overmorrow

Arachnapocalypse! The Anthology

Once Upon a WolfPack

Available at your favorite online retailer.

ABOUT CW HAWES

CW Hawes has written over 50 novels and shorter works of fiction. He was also an award-winning poet and had over 200 poems appear in ezines and and print.

He is a founding member of the Underground Authors and was the impetus for the highly successful Magnolia Bluff Crime Chronicles series.

After 35 years of working in county government, he retired at the beginning of 2015 and began a second career as a fictioneer. Perhaps some of the horrors Pierce Mostyn faces can be traced to his creator's own experiences in county government and beyond. Perhaps.

CW lives in Southern California. He enjoys reading, writing, chess and other board games, his daily morning walk, and contemplating the meaning of life while smoking his pipe. He also hasn't met a doughnut or a pizza he doesn't like, is something of a tea snob, and rocks out to Handel and Vaughan Williams.

You can get curated content and the occasional free story when you join his mailing list, and you can reach him at his website, on X, and also Facebook.

To join his mailing list, click, tap, or scan the QR code:

To visit him on his website, click, tap, or scan the QR code:

To visit him on X, click, tap, or scan the QR code:

To visit him on Facebook, click, tap, or scan the QR code: